*boy*genius
A NOVEL BY
YONGSOO PARK

Akashic Books
New York

Published by Akashic Books
©2002 Yongsoo Park
Layout by Sohrab Habibion

ISBN: 1-888451-24-6
Library of Congress Control Number: 2001097215
All rights reserved
First printing
Printed in Canada

Akashic Books
PO Box 1456
New York, NY 10009
Akashic7@aol.com
www.akashicbooks.com

Acknowledgments

This book is dedicated to So Jene, whose infinite love, patience, understanding, and generosity of spirit made it possible. She is my inspiration, guide, and voice of sanity.

I'd also like to thank my parents, who taught me the valuable lesson of courage and perseverance; and my brother, who is a beacon of strength.

Lastly, I'd like to thank Johnny Temple, Ibrahim Ahmad, and everyone at Akashic Books for their proven commitment to publishing fresh voices.

BOOK I
Rabbit Peninsula

CHAPTER 1
Commie Bastard

In the beginning there was His Excellency the Most Honorable President Park, who created the heavens and the earth and saw that it was good. Then came the dragon, not an overweight Western dragon, but a magnificent fire-breathing dragon of the Orient, born of a snake who, through sheer will and stubbornness, outslithered death for 5,000 years. Nine months before my birth, Father dreamt that just such a dragon soared out of the East Korean Sea, flew six circles above Mount Nam, then disappeared under Mother's satin hanbok.

Despite this magnificent vision, little in my first years distinguished me from the other infants in the peninsula. I cried when I was hungry and slept when I was tired. I cherished the warmth of my mother's round nipple; and my first words, like those of every healthy baby in the land, were "Long Live His Excellency the Most Honorable President Park."

Everything changed the summer I turned three, when His Excellency launched the Great Search for Genius Campaign. To identify future pillars of society who would help drive communists back to the Yalu, every child from the tiniest hamlet to the largest city was given the Great Search for Genius test. When my score proved to be the highest in the land, my photograph was featured on the front page of *Korea Tomorrow*, *Korea Today*, and *Korea Yesterday*; and I was paraded before every living room through my own KBS television show, *The Boy Genius Hour*, brought to the people by Lotte Confectioners and Haitai Detergent. I starred in the show alongside Choco Joe, an American G.I. whose skin was as black and glistening as the shiniest eggplant. Wearing a pair of red boxing shorts, he imitated animal sounds and played catchy melodies on his rusty harmonica. Together, we taught school-children from Pusan to Seoul the A-B-C's and English phrases like "Commie bastards must be killed without mercy," "His Excellency the Most Honorable President Park speaks the will of the people," and "The U.S.A. is our number-one friend and ally in everything."

No one knew for sure just how old Choco Joe was or how he'd come to be at KBS. Not even Mr. K, the show's producer who'd been at the station since the end of the Korean War, remembered the circumstances surrounding Choco Joe's entry into Korean showbiz. But there were rumors. Some said he'd been a lounge singer in Hawaii who'd had to flee insurmountable gambling debts. Others claimed that he was a veteran of the Korean War who'd fallen under the spell of our nation's breathtaking natural beauty. Still others intimated that Choco Joe was a CIA operative who'd been sent to monitor our actions. I didn't pay these rumors any mind. I didn't care how old Choco Joe was or how he'd come to be with us. To me, he was simply a friend, with whom I could smoke and curse freely.

Choco Joe and I spent many hours together during the long lulls in between taping in a forgotten basement storage room. There, we busied ourselves by reenacting elaborate fight sequences from chopsocky Hong Kong kung fu films. When we grew tired of that, Choco Joe taught me English idioms that couldn't be found in the language tapes issued by the Education Ministry like "motherfuckin' ho," "punk-ass bitch," and "no-good honkey bastard."

One afternoon, after we'd finished taping the first half of a three-hour Christmas special, Choco Joe moved the old boxes that cluttered the storage room and cleared a small space the size of a practice seereum ring. Then, he turned to me solemnly and said, "Boy Genius, I think it's time I showed you how to defend yourself against no-good punks if ever you find yourself stranded in a North American ghetto."

He let out a loud taekwondo cry and jumped three feet straight up in the air. At the crest of this trajectory, he thrust his right leg high above him and spun 720 degrees sideways. When he finally returned to the ground, he struck the cement floor with just his index and middle fingers, boring two clean holes, each eight centimeters deep.

My jaw dropped and I began clapping. He smiled and said, "Now it's your turn."

I stood up and mimicked his movements as best as I could, jumping as high as I could and striking phantom enemies that emerged from behind dusty stacks of old videotapes. But my chubby body wasn't ready for Choco Joe's ancient Shaolin techniques, and after just ten seconds, I plopped back down on a cardboard box, out of breath and hungry for rest.

Choco Joe frowned. "You gotta shape up, kid. *Mens sana in corpore sano.* That's Latin for get off your fat ass and swing your arms once in a while."

I wiped the sweat off my forehead. "Don't be like that, Choco Joe. We're friends, remember? Sit down and have a cigarette with me."

He grumbled, then sat down next to me, stretching out his long bony legs and smoothing out the wrinkles on his shiny red shorts. His ankles were thin and his shins were covered with thick wooly tufts of hair. He handed me a Lucky Strike and lit another for himself. "It's a good thing I like you, kid. I don't know why, but I do."

After a few puffs, I said, "Tell me more about America, Choco Joe."

"It's nothing like here, that's for sure."

"How are things different?"

He tilted his head back and blew two perfect smoke rings in quick succession. The rings floated up toward the dozen exposed pipes that crisscrossed the ceiling, then came together to form the outline of the continental U.S.

"How'd you do that?" I said, pointing to Texas, which was my favorite state because it was home to cowboys, rustlers, and wild mustangs.

Choco Joe smiled. "It's an old trick I learned back in the States. Just mind over matter."

The map dissolved away. Choco Joe leaned his head back and folded his hands behind his neck. "You wanted to know how the U.S. is different from here, right?"

"Right."

"First of all, I'd never be on a TV show in the U.S. At least not on one like *The Boy Genius Hour.*"

"Why not?"

He flicked the ash from his cigarette on the floor. "It's too complicated to get into right now. There are conspiracies on top of conspiracies. But that's an entirely different can of beans. For now, I'll focus on the obvious. First, every major city in the good old U.S. of A. has a ballpark. And I'm not talking about some dinky sandlot next to a junkyard or a rice paddy. I'm talking about a legitimate goodness-to-gracious genuine authenticated architectural monument dedicated to the best game that man ever invented."

"Is it true that every house in America has a lawn?"

He chuckled. "Did Mr. K tell you that?"

I nodded. Mr. K often went abroad for business and was our resident expert on the 101 differences between the U.S. and our homeland. One difference was that we ate dogs while Americans treated them like children. Another difference was that we wore white at funerals while they wore black.

"Mr. K's not a hundred-percent correct, but he's pretty damn close. Not every house there has a lawn, and not everyone lives in a house. But there's more green in the U.S. of A. than there is in any city here, kid. And trees in America are big, not sad little saplings you got here that pass for vegetation. There are trees there that are twice as old as your country."

"But Korea is more than 5,000 years old."

"The trees are called redwoods and they're older than

14

that. They're in California, and they're bigger than this building. Shoot, just about everything's bigger back in the States. There are cornfields in Missouri bigger than South and North Korea combined."

"Is that where you're from, Choco Joe? Missouri?"

"Yup. St. Louis, Missouri. The best city in the world. You really owe it to yourself to check it out sometime, kid. It's the best city in all of America. There's even an arch there in my honor."

"His Excellency's going to build a bullet train that'll connect Seoul to Pusan. It's going to ferry people at speeds of up to 200 kilometers per hour."

"Two hundred kilometers? What's that? About 120 miles?"

"124.274."

"Not bad. They got guys in the majors who can throw almost that fast. Shoot, if it weren't for my bum knee I might have had a shot in the majors. A couple of scouts from the Braves looked at me a few times when I was a kid. I was pretty good then. Who knows? If A-B-C had happened instead of X-Y-Z, I mighta been teammates with Hank Aaron. But then again, if that had happened, I probably wouldn't be here talking with you now, right?"

"I wish you could have played with Hank Aaron."

"Forget it, kid. It's all in the past. All I know is that there's nothing like baseball in the summertime. The only thing that's better is girls in see-through dresses. I'm only telling you this 'cuz you're a genius, kid, but girls in America got curves and moves you just can't begin to comprehend. I'm talking 'bout moves that defy all known laws of physics and pure math."

"Do you think I could play for the Braves some day?"

"I'm not gonna lie to you, kid. I don't know if you'd get to play for the Braves or any other team in the majors. That all depends on whether you got the stuff or not. But there are other things besides baseball. And a kid like you, I think you'd fit in real nice over there."

"You really think so, Choco Joe?"

He nodded firmly and said, "Sure, kid. With your guts and

brains, you'd make out like Jesse James." He then pointed his fingers like guns, shot off two imaginary bullets, and winked at me.

I nearly jumped up for joy, but just then, the door swung open and Mr. K stepped inside. He had on his white linen suit, a red bow tie, and black-and-white golf shoes. It was his usual outfit. Behind him stood a man in a black suit whose face was covered in shadow.

Something about this man compelled Choco Joe and me to stub out our cigarettes and stand up straight.

Mr. K shot us a dirty look anyway, then said, "Boy Genius, an important person has come to see you."

The man in the black suit stepped toward me, and his face came into full view. His features were nondescript, almost peasant-like, except that the letters H-I-J were scarred thick and red across his left cheek. He stared at me for a long time and said nothing.

To ease the awkwardness that quickly filled the room, Mr. K stroked my head as if I were a favorite pet and said, "Boy Genius has been a godsend for KBS. He gets over three thousand fan letters a day. Of course, he doesn't have the time to read and respond to each letter. But we make sure every fan gets a photograph of him. That's the least we could do for our biggest star."

The man with the scar nodded politely, then took out a small square envelope from the inside pocket of his suit. He handed it to me, and, without another word, turned around and started for the door.

Mr. K followed him to the door and bowed after him obsequiously, lowering his torso below his waist. Then, just as abruptly as he had come into our world, the man in the black suit was gone.

I stood there, holding the envelope.

"Well? Aren't you going to open it?" Mr. K asked, rushing over to me.

I ripped the envelope open and took out its content, a square piece of laminated cardboard with my name embossed in gold across the top in masterful Chinese calligraphy. Across the bottom of the square were the words: "You are cordially invited to the Blue House to welcome in His Excellency's Fifth Republic."

My hands trembled and blood rushed to my cheeks. I felt faint and quickly sat down.

Mr. K snatched the invitation from me and ran his fingers slowly over it as if he hoped good chi would rub off on him. Then, he said, "No one from this station has ever been invited to the Blue House for New Year's Eve in all the years I've been here. This is a great honor, Boy Genius. Not just for you, but for all of KBS."

Choco Joe tousled my hair gently and said, "Look at that, Boy Genius. You're a VIP now!"

It was both a joke and the truth. Only 100 people were invited to the New Year's Eve Gala at the Blue House. An invitation was proof that one had reached the pinnacle of his field.

I took the invitation back from Mr. K, then turned to Choco Joe. "You think I could have another cigarette, Choco Joe?"

Mr. K gave Choco Joe a dirty look, but he gave me a cigarette anyway. I took a long drag and blew out a thick cloud of smoke. The smoke floated up toward the ceiling and formed the visage of His Excellency. It was the same handsome countenance that graced the cover of every schoolbook, the front of every postage stamp, and the dreams of every loyal citizen.

Immediately, Mr. K, a decorated veteran of the ROK Army, slapped his feet together and stood at attention. He then saluted the visage and began singing the national anthem.

I ran my fingers over the invitation again. The paper felt hot as if it were burning, and the thick letters seemed to be glowing of their own light. Behind me, Mr. K's rich baritone echoed, "From the East Sea to Mount Baekdu . . ."

CHAPTER 2
Five-Year Plan

On New Year's Eve, a blizzard engineered by a team of North Korean alchemists who had no qualms about using knowledge for evil dropped ninety centimeters of snow on our capital. Roads were closed and the three bridges that spanned the majestic Han were declared impassable. But nothing could keep me away from the chance to see His Excellency in person. Sporting my junior military fatigues and combat boots, I waded through the snow to the Blue House, the only residence in the land allowed by the Constitution to have 100 rooms. The building sat on top of a hill overlooking the capital. On both sides of the road, pine branches weighed down by snow jutted out at odd angles. According to local lore, each twisted branch represented the pain and heartache suffered by a child who'd lost his mother in the war.

At the Blue House gate, two armed sentries in military fatigues frisked me carefully from head to toe, then escorted me across the vast Blue House lawn. High above the Blue House, our flag fluttered majestically against the night sky. A clean white rectangle with a blue and red yin and yang symbol in the center and four sets of black lines on the corners, it was a marvelous amalgam of the old and new, and the perfect symbol of what His Excellency wished for our nation, a delicate balance of tradition and modernization. After pausing briefly to salute the flag, I hurried up the stairs and stepped inside the Hall of Patriots.

Just inside the entrance, Our Most Virtuous First Lady, a saint who always wore an immaculate white hanbok, and her three beautiful children, Harmonious Sisters Keun-hye and Keun-yong, and Courageous Younger Brother Chi-Man, welcomed me and bowed in unison. Then, Our Most Virtuous First Lady smiled gloriously and said, "We're so pleased to have you join us tonight, Boy Genius. Thank you so much for coming."

Her voice and movement meshed perfectly together, and I couldn't help but stand back and admire her grace and elegance. She was truly the perfect role model for every woman in the land. I saluted her and said, "The honor and privilege is all mine."

The Hall of Patriots had been transformed into a stunning Parisian ballroom for the evening's festivities. A thousand diamonds glistened from a hundred chandeliers. The KBS Quartet played in the front of the hall and festive music filled the air. Handsome men dressed in fine tuxedos danced and conversed with elegant women in stunning evening gowns.

Twenty tables sat in the back of the hall. In the center of every table, there was a life-sized bust of His Excellency carved in ice. I went to my assigned table and sat down next to Sohn Ki Chung, a national hero who had captured gold in the marathon at the 1936 Berlin Olympic Games, a decade before the yoke of colonialism had been lifted from our necks.

He tousled my hair and said, "Do you know that my grandchildren are crazy about you?"

"Thank you," I said.

"But you really should exercise a little. Being chubby is okay when you're a boy, but you won't stay young forever. What I'd recommend is a rigorous program of jogging and taekwondo. And most importantly, you must stay away from ice cream. Ice cream will destroy your body more quickly than the most lethal virus."

I didn't need to be reminded yet again that I carried a few extra pounds. So I nodded politely, then promptly turned to my left to Cha Bum Geun, the captain of our national soccer team. Mr. Cha had led our nation to numerous victories over the Japanese in international competitions and was our only hope of someday capturing the World Cup. In lieu of a greeting, he rolled up his sleeve, flexed his right bicep, and said, "Boy Genius, do you think you could take some time to speak to my son? He's been having some trouble at school, and I think he might be hanging out with the wrong crowd."

"Have him contact me at KBS," I said, trying to sound sympathetic, though I knew full well that the only thing I would do for the boy is have Mr. K give him a quick tour and a souvenir photo.

Some minutes later, the KBS Quartet stopped playing and all eyes turned to the front of the hall. But instead of His Excellency, out stepped Yi Mee-Ja, a ballad singer who was everyone's favorite despite her homely looks. Her voice made people remember all the sadness that had ever crossed their lives. For Father, her voice evoked memories of his childhood when all he ever wished for was enough rice to put in his shrunken belly. For Mother, her songs brought back memories of swimming across the Han River in the dead of night while commie bastards chased her with machine guns.

As Ms. Yi sang, women dabbed their tears with handkerchiefs while men sighed forlornly and stared at the floor. In the middle of this sea of emotion, I felt nothing. My thoughts were only with one person, His Excellency the Most Honorable President Park, the valiant knight who had single-handedly rescued our nation from the Four Evils: poverty, anarchy, corruption, and communism.

At exactly one minute into the New Year, a ton of shiny confetti rained down on us from the ceiling, and Mr. Sohn and Mr. Cha both wished me a prosperous new year. I wished them the same, then skulked away toward the bathroom, kicking the mounds of confetti that had piled up on the floor. Another year had gone by without my meeting His Excellency in person.

As I relieved myself in a urinal, two men in black suits who needed no introduction—their every movement announced their membership in the KCIA—sidled up next to me. Without a word, they led me down a long underground passageway that twisted and turned for what seemed like numerous kilometers. As we walked, all I could hear was the echoing of their footsteps, solid and precise after what I imagined must have been years of rigorous practice.

We stopped at the end of a long corridor. There, standing in front of a bamboo door, was the man with the scar who had delivered the invitation to me at KBS. Without a word or a trace of recognition, he pulled the door open slowly, then nudged me gently inside.

The door creaked shut behind me. The room was dark, but soon a figure slumped in a large chair with his back to me became visible. The figure was staring out a tall window that looked out at the constellations of light shining from the capital. Between the figure and me, there was a long desk that spanned nearly the entire length of the room.

After a long moment, the figure said, "I lifted the curfew to let them welcome in the New Year. They're out there now, celebrating despite the snow."

His voice was soft but commanding, and I knew then that I was in the presence of His Excellency the Most Honorable President Park. He swiveled slowly around in His chair and peered at me through the large mirror-faced aviator sunglasses that had been surgically attached to His face. In them, I could see my own reflection. To my great shame, I looked even smaller and more cowardly than I felt.

My knees trembled and my entire body started to itch. Despite my genius, I didn't know how I ought to behave or speak. Upset at my inability to make a strong first impression, I did what every boy in my peninsula would have done. I stood up straight, clicked my boots together, and saluted Him.

He nodded slightly, then said, "At ease, son." He then pointed to a chair opposite Him.

The invitation was timely. I collapsed into the chair and prayed that my nervousness would not betray me during the most momentous meeting of my young life.

"Have you had a chance to meet my children?" He asked.

"Yes, Your Excellency. They're fine children. Brave and intelligent. The best children in the land."

He chuckled. "They're good kids. Not brilliant like you, of course. But they're humble and they work hard. I'm very proud of them. They've always attended public schools. I don't want them to grow up arrogant or spoiled. They have to learn that they're no better or worse than their compatriots."

"The Great Kon-Fu-Tze praised the virtues of humility and diligence, Your Excellency. Both are qualities that have been extolled by great thinkers of the East and West. A prime example can be found in the Tale of Three Kingdoms, where three great generals seeking to unite warring kingdoms displayed humility toward their troops."

He chuckled again, then reached across the table and held up a pack of cigarettes. I didn't know whether to take one. Smoking in front of an elder, especially one of His Excellency's magnitude, was a clear breech of the rules of etiquette set out by the Great Kon-Fu-Tze. On the other hand, I craved a smoke and I couldn't say no to His Excellency.

As if sensing my discomfort and anxiety, He said, "It's okay, Boy Genius. I know you have a fondness for Lucky Strikes. And anyway, you're almost a man."

With that, His Excellency wiped away all my nervousness and I felt as if I were in the storage room back at KBS. I took a cigarette, and His Excellency and I smoked together like two old friends.

After a few puffs, His Excellency leaned across the table and said, "I heard that you met with the people from Guinness last month. How did that go?"

"They're going to list me in their book as having the world's highest I.Q., Your Excellency."

He clapped His hands together. "That's fantastic, Boy Genius. Just fantastic."

"It's a small achievement compared to all that Your Excellency has done, but I'm happy that Your Excellency is pleased."

"Don't be so modest, Boy Genius. You've done a great thing for our country. A truly great thing. China has produced many geniuses over the years, and so has Japan and India. Even the Philippines has produced a few people of semi-genius status, but our country hasn't seen a true genius for many years. Not since the days of old when Admiral Yi-Sun-Shin guarded our shores with a fleet of turtle ships. He was a genius of the highest order, doubly remarkable because he combined both thought and action. Times have changed, I'm afraid. Now, our young people have to be forced to sit at their desks to pursue knowledge and learning. Left on their own, I'm afraid they would rather shoot marbles and chase after dragonflies. But you've changed all that. You're showing the world that we as a people are capable of great things. You're inspiring our young people to cultivate their minds. You're making our nation proud again, Boy Genius. For this, I thank you."

I didn't know what to say. Even as my mind raced faster than the speed of light to wargame a brilliant response that would demonstrate my love, my loyalty, and my genius, I knew in my heart that no amount of genius could shine in the light of His own. Like the genius of Admiral Yi, His Excellency's was a brilliance that combined action, will, and history itself. Après moi, there would be many geniuses, but after Him, there would be nothing but chaos and poverty.

Suddenly, a worried look came over His Excellency and He sighed softly.

"Is anything the matter, Your Excellency?" I asked.

He smiled gently and said, "You may not be aware of this, Boy Genius, but not all is well in our beloved home. As strange as it may seem, there are workers who refuse to work and students who'd rather march in the streets than devote themselves to their studies. Of course, this is due largely to the communist infiltration of our universities, but we can't ignore the fact that there are some who are genuinely disinclined to become productive members of society. Then, there are those politicians and journalists who say my policies

are antiquated and unwise. There are even some in my very administration who secretly pray for nothing less than my demise."

"You mustn't fret, Your Excellency. These problems are mere
trifles. They can be dealt with and solved."

He smiled. "Thank you, Boy Genius. Your reassurance means
a lot. But I'm afraid not everyone shares your view. The students
who are protesting are still a minority, but there's no guarantee
that their number will not grow in the future or that their parents
will not join them one day."

"Without Your Excellency's strong leadership, the nation will
return once again to the wretched state it was once in.
Corruption will again pervade every facet of society. Millions will
be driven to the streets, and the capital will again be filled with
beggars, cripples, drug addicts, and orphans."

"Yes, I'm afraid this is true."

"The people are clamoring for change, Your Excellency. So
give them what they want."

"Just like that?" He said, shaking His head as if in disbelief.
"Give them change? You say that as though change were some
worthless trifle peddled at the East Gate Market. Change only
comes with hard work or the blood of many people. It's not doled
out like sacks of cabbages to just anybody who thinks they want it."

"Your Excellency is perfectly correct, but what I'm suggesting
is a different kind of change."

He flicked the ash from His cigarette into a celadon ashtray.
"What do you mean?"

"Cosmetic change, Your Excellency. The most superficial kind
of change there is. Abolish the midnight curfew so that young
men can roam the streets all night in a drunken stupor instead of
thinking about their lives. Abolish school uniforms and ease the
curriculum so that students will feel free in their blue jeans and
their parents will think change has come. Expand television pro-
grams so that the masses can watch soap operas twenty-four hours
a day instead of milling about on street corners entertaining
thoughts of revolution. And lastly, give the masses professional

sports. Baseball, a game of percentages, would be particularly well-suited to our disposition, but other diversions would do just as well. Taken as a whole, these reforms are small and utterly cosmetic, but they will endear you to the people and to the outside world, especially the Americans. For as you well know, the Americans are our best friends whether we like it or not."

"Our best friends whether we like it or not," He repeated, as a look of amusement came over Him. "You're even more clever than I'd hoped, Boy Genius. It's clear that you have a firm grasp on geopolitics and history. However, your suggestions about cosmetic change worry me. They may make sense in theory, but they underestimate our citizenry. You give them too little credit. Our citizens are not the mindless, spineless mob you make them out to be, Boy Genius. You forget that it was they who fought against the Japanese, and it was they who overthrew the corrupt regimes of my predecessors. We must not underestimate their true capabilities."

"I didn't mean to do so, Your Excellency," I said, staring at the edge of the desk.

"Don't feel bad, Boy Genius. Your suggestions have more substance than those from my entire Cabinet. That's quite an accomplishment. And I will consider them seriously."

"Thank you, Your Excellency."

"You're quite welcome. Now promise me something, Boy Genius."

"Yes, Your Excellency."

"Promise me that you will always use your mind for the glory and prosperity of our country. Even when I'm not around to remind you of this."

I looked Him straight in the eye and said, "I will always use my mind for the glory and prosperity of our beloved nation, Your Excellency. Even when You're not around to remind me of this. I promise You with all my heart and love for all the days of my life."

I would have promised Him anything. He was the father I had always dreamed should have been my own.

CHAPTER 3
Fatherland Liberation War

Everyone was abuzz when I returned to KBS to tape the New Year's Day special. The receptionist greeted me with a bigger smile than usual and the staff members shot me furtive looks of awe and envy. Mr. K was in a particularly good mood and bounced about the studio with more energy than he'd ever had. Every time he happened to be near me, he pinched my cheeks and said, "What I wouldn't give to have a pretty daughter so I could have you as a son-in-law."

No one came out and said it outright, but I knew that their unusual behavior was a direct result of my having attended the Blue House Gala. A photograph of me standing with Our Most Virtuous First Lady had appeared on the front page of that day's *Korea Today*. I didn't mind the fuss at all. Despite my genius, I was still a little boy. I had done something special, and I wanted to be recognized for it.

At the first break in taping, I rushed to the storage room and told Choco Joe all about my meeting with His Excellency.

"You really talked to him about baseball?" Choco Joe asked, unable to hide his astonishment.

"Sure. And His Excellency said I was more clever than He'd hoped."

I then leaned my head back and blew a perfect smoke ring. It floated slowly toward the ceiling and turned into a reproduction of the photograph from *Korea Today*.

"It's amazing, Boy Genius. Simply amazing," said Choco Joe. I wasn't sure whether he was referring to my smoke sculpture or my meeting with His Excellency.

"Wouldn't it be great if we really got professional baseball, Choco Joe? Then you and I could go to games together. I don't know if they'd have hot dogs, but we could eat dried cuttlefish. That'd be good too, wouldn't it, Choco Joe?"

"Sure, kid. Sure. If we get professional baseball here, I'll take you to the games and eat a dozen dried cuttlefish."

"I hope it happens, Choco Joe. I really do." I could already picture Choco Joe and me hanging out at the ballpark, chewing on cuttlefish and drinking soda pop.

"If it does, we'll owe it all to you, kid. You really are a genius."

"Thanks, Choco Joe."

Just then, the door swung open and Mr. K rushed inside. He turned to me and said, "Boy Genius, there's someone waiting for you outside."

I glanced at Choco Joe. He just shrugged his shoulders. I turned and started for the door.

CHAPTER 4

$$a2 + b2 = c2$$

A glistening black sedan from Deutschland was waiting for me in the parking lot. As I approached the car, the passenger door swung open slowly. H-I-J was sitting in the back seat with his head staring straight ahead. He remained silent and motionless even when I got inside and sat down next to him.

The driver, an elderly man with white gloves, put the car in gear and we were off. In no time, we were racing alongside the glistening waters of the Han, whose energy His Excellency was planning to harness with the construction of three hydroelectric power plants.

Without ever turning toward me, H-I-J said, "You've made quite an impression on His Excellency. He's been telling everyone what a brilliant boy you are."

It was the first time I'd heard him speak. His voice was monotone and robotic, but there was no way I could miss the way he'd deliberately stressed the word "brilliant."

I nodded and said nothing.

"I understand you even got to smoke with him." He paused as if waiting for me to say something. When I didn't, he continued, "I've known His Excellency for sixteen years now, and I've yet to have the privilege of smoking with him. You're a very lucky boy. I just hope you never disappoint him. For your sake and his."

The envy in his voice told me not to say anything, so I turned to the window and stared at the river. Along the river's edge, clusters of women with white handkerchiefs tied around their heads were crouched on their haunches doing the laundry as their ancestors had done for thousands of years. Just a hundred yards away to their left, a thousand bow-legged laborers were climbing up impossibly tall bamboo scaffolding to weld the metal skeleton of a luxury thirty-story apartment building. As I stared at these agile workers climbing up toward the sky, I wondered which part of the river Mother had crossed to flee communists during the war.

CHAPTER 5

G.J. Kim

Three armed soldiers with machine guns slung on their shoulders waved us through the Blue House Gate. From the way they all favored their left legs, it was obvious that they, like His Excellency and my father, were men of humble beginnings from North Kyoungsang Province.

I followed H-I-J silently down a different set of winding corridors to the familiar bamboo door. As before, H-I-J opened it, nudged me inside, then quietly shut the door behind me.

His Excellency was standing with His back to me, staring out the tall windows that faced out at the capital. Thanks to the light shining through the window, I was able to see more detail of the room than I had on my previous visit. Thick volumes of classic Chinese texts filled the tall bookshelves that stood against the side walls. Next to one shelf, there was a large scroll featuring the Chinese pictogram for "will," written in powerful yet gentle strokes.

After a long silence, His Excellency said, without turning around, "It looks like the skeleton of a prehistoric animal, doesn't it?"

It was a strange comment, and it took me a few seconds to realize that He was talking about the same construction site that I had passed along the river. I stepped closer to Him and peered out the window for a better look. Perhaps it was the change in vantage point, but the bamboo scaffolding and the metal frame of the building did look very much like the skeleton of an ancient animal.

Without ever taking his eyes off the building, His Excellency continued, "No dinosaur bones have ever been found in our country, Boy Genius, but according to the writings of our ancient scholars, the foothills of Mount Baekdu were once teeming with dragons. Some people dismiss these accounts as mere myth, but I am not one of them. I believe in dragons. To lead a country like ours, one must believe in them."

"I believe in dragons too, Your Excellency."

"Do you know that our mountains were once filled with great tigers?"

"Yes, Your Excellency." It was a fact that every schoolboy knew by heart.

"Today, tigers only exist in our zoos. And even those have to be imported from foreign countries, but it wasn't always that way. There was a time when tigers roamed freely in our mountains, and villagers had to travel in large groups out of fear of a tiger attack. But all that changed with the coming of the Japanese. Japanese hunters traveled up and down the peninsula to wipe out tigers from our country. Some people think this was simply the act of overzealous hunters, but this isn't so. It was a deliberate and calculated policy of the Japanese Colonial Administration. It was believed that by wiping out tigers from Korea, our spirit would be weakened and we would lose our will to fight for independence."

"We suffered greatly under the Japanese, Your Excellency."

He nodded slightly. "As a boy, I once saw a tiger that three Japanese hunters had killed in the mountains near my village. Its carcass was huge, as big as an ox. It took twelve men to carry this carcass to the nearest railroad station. The village elders warned the men not to do this job, but they did not listen. It is said that the hide of every tiger killed in our country was sent back to Japan and sewn together into a large mosaic that formed the map of Asia. It is rumored that this was then given to the Emperor, who hung it up in his study. Some scholars might characterize Japan's chasing after our tigers as a senseless action driven by superstition, but these scholars don't realize how clever the Japanese mind truly is. For better or for worse, I know the Japanese better than they know themselves. You see, when I was your age, there was no country called Korea. We were all subjects of the Emperor."

"It was a terrible chapter in our history, Your Excellency."

"That is true. But there are lessons to be learned. It's wrong to place the blame of our colonization only with the Japanese. We as a people and as a nation are just as deserving of blame. Of course, my critics will tell you that I've been influenced too much by the Japanese. They will cite my record of service in the Japanese military and fault me for opening diplomatic relations with a former colonizer. These men would prefer that our two nations remain sworn enemies for eternity. But these critics are blinded, Boy Genius. As ruthless and despicable as the Japanese are, there are things we must learn from them. While our mighty kings sought foolishly to preserve the past and indulge their whims, Japan opened its shores to new ideas and embraced change. They modernized their economy and their military. They crushed Russia, then considered to be a military superpower, in the biggest war the world had seen, then just four decades later dared to wage war against America. Their eventual defeat is almost immaterial. The fact that a tiny Asian country, peopled by a race of people perceived by the West to be weak and inferior, did not cower to the West, proved to the U.S. and all the world that they are a nation to be reckoned with. Their strength and spirit is visible even today. Out of the ashes of war, they have risen like a phoenix to conquer the world as an economic power. They have rebuilt their cities and now live better than most Europeans. We must do the same. But first, we must learn to come together as a nation and act in unison."

He turned around, picked up a newspaper from His desk, and handed it to me. It was a copy of the *Washington Post* folded to an article with the headline "ROK MP DENOUNCES INJUSTICE."

According to the article, a congressman from Kwangju had met with foreign reporters while vacationing in Japan and criticized His Excellency for exercising what he termed "unhealthy control over the nation's press and media."

"I'm sorry, Your Excellency," I said, setting the paper back on His desk.

"It's not your fault, Boy Genius. Not everyone has the best interest of our nation at heart. This opportunist has tarnished our nation's integrity to get his name in this worthless rag of American propaganda. It doesn't seem like much of a trade in my book, but he obviously thinks otherwise. What is it about us as a people that drives us to help our enemies kill our tigers, Boy Genius? Can you figure it out?"

I remained silent. I didn't know the answer.

"Whatever challenges we face, we face together as a nation, a family. After all, we are a nation of cousins, are we not?"

"We are all cousins, Your Excellency."

His Excellency sighed. "Maybe I'm being too harsh. After all, these foreigners are also to blame. They profess outwardly to promote independence and democracy, but what they really want is a colony they can call their own. Of course, they would never admit this. To them, we're simply beneficiaries of their generosity. They conveniently forget that we provide a strategic military base. We purchase tons of American goods, and we've already sent 50,000 soldiers to fight their war in Vietnam. Sometimes, I think we'd be better off without their aid, but then I see the poverty in our streets."

I stepped closer to Him. "Your Excellency, it's clear that the Americans think they can champion this lying dog against You. But we can show them who has the will of the people, and we can make sure the miscreant never dares again to speak against our homeland."

"What do you suggest, Boy Genius?"

"We must put a scare into the miscreant, Your Excellency. A scare that will insure that he will never again forget his place in our glorious nation of 5,000 years. A scare that will forever remind him that no matter what sweet things these foreigners whisper in his ears, his cousins do not live in Washington, D.C., but in our peninsula."

"Go on."

When I finished telling Him the details of my plan, His Excellency smiled and said, "Again you are at my side in this time of trouble. You're loyal to the end, Boy Genius, and I will never forget your loyalty."

I bowed deeply. "It is my duty, Your Excellency, and my privilege."

CHAPTER 6
To Hell With Babe Ruth

Three days later, the miscreant appeared on television holding up copies of the *New York Times* and the *Washington Post*. "A whale with pro-democratic tendencies swallowed me and carried me to an isolated beach near Ulsan. There, a kind fisherman found me and carried me in his rickshaw to the hospital."

A hundred flashbulbs clicked and the camera zoomed in closer. The headlines on both front pages shouted: "WHALE SAVES BEACON OF HUMAN RIGHTS!"

He then said, "I was dangled outside the KCIA boat through the tsunami waves."

"You believe what this guy went through?" said Choco Joe, pointing to the small black-and-white TV he'd set up in our hangout. "If it wasn't for us Americans, this guy would be dead right now."

I knew otherwise. The miscreant had been abducted by the KCIA and dangled outside a fishing boat. The Americans tracked him with a powerful spotlight from a helicopter, blaring, "We see you and we know what you're doing. We're filming everything." But the miscreant didn't owe his life to the Americans. His Excellency had merely spared him because he was no longer a threat. No matter how brave the miscreant tried to appear in public, he now knew the lesson known by every child in the land—all life in our peninsula belonged to His Excellency the Most Honorable President Park.

"Can you keep a secret?" I said to Choco Joe.

"Sure, kid."

When I finished telling him about what had prompted the

35

miscreant's abduction and who was really responsible for keeping the man alive, he shook his head slowly and said, "I don't know, kid. I know you're awful smart, but this doesn't sound good. Not good at all. I think you might be forgetting that we're entertainers."

It wasn't the reaction I'd wanted or expected from him. "What d'you mean?" I said.

"Entertaining is one thing. Getting involved with politics is an entirely different can of beans, kid. You oughta know that."

"But it's our duty to serve our country, Choco Joe."

He got up and started pacing the room. "I still don't like it, kid. Entertainment is entertainment, and politics is politics. And the two should never meet. That's the first code of show biz."

"I don't know why you're getting so worked up about this, Choco Joe. I just gave His Excellency my opinion because He asked me for it. Anyway, the bastard deserved it. He traded in the good name of our country just to get his name in a worthless rag of American propaganda."

"American propaganda?" he said, raising his voice. "You're starting to scare me, kid."

"Why? Because I'm speaking the truth?"

"Listen, kid. I know you're a genius, but the *New York Times* and the *Washington Post* are not vehicles of American propaganda. They're just newspapers that report the news."

"Of course you'd say that. You're an American."

"Fine, kid. How 'bout this? Would you say that *Korea Today* or *Korea Tomorrow* are there to promote Korean propaganda?"

"It's not the same thing."

"Why not?"

"*Korea Today* isn't written by CIA agents posing as journalists."

He shook his head. "Fine. Forget that stuff about propaganda. Just listen to this. Politics can destroy lives, kid. Politics can destroy otherwise perfectly good careers."

I rolled my eyes. "Choco Joe, you sound like some old lady

who's afraid to cross the street."

He wagged a finger at me. "You say that now, kid. But you mark my word. I've seen it happen plenty of times, completely happy entertainers whose lives get turned upside down 'cuz some bureaucrat had an axe to grind or some bigwig didn't like the entertainer's jokes. Trust me, kid. It's not a pretty sight when that happens."

"But I just told you His Excellency's on my side. And you saw how Mr. K and the others were on New Year's. How's all that a bad thing?"

"Come on, kid. They don't care about you. They're only thinking about themselves. You're old enough to know that." He stubbed out his cigarette on the floor and said, "Listen, kid. I know you think His Excellency's the greatest person who ever lived, but you gotta remember that not everyone's as crazy about him as you are."

"But if it weren't for His Excellency, North Korea would invade us at this very moment. His Excellency's the only person keeping us safe."

"Trust me on this, kid. Not everyone's as big a fan of His Excellency as you. There are lots of people who wouldn't mind if he decided to retire."

I stood up. "Name one person."

"What?"

"Go ahead. I dare you. Name one person."

"Listen, kid. I'm not gonna sit here and name names."

"Because you can't."

"That's not it. Because I don't want to. And I don't have to. But trust me on this, kid. There are people out there who wouldn't mind it one bit if he suddenly disappeared."

I was at a loss for words. The mere idea of a world without His Excellency was sickening. I stared at Choco Joe for a long while in silence. His feet and his boxing gloves both suddenly seemed way too big for him, and it dawned on me that Choco Joe might not be the happy-go-lucky American he appeared to be.

Exercising extreme caution, I leaned toward him and whispered, "You're not a communist, are you, Choco Joe?"

He shut his eyes for a moment, then chuckled. "No, kid. I'm not a communist."

"You're sure?"

"Yes, I'm sure. I'm not a communist and I never have been one."

"Even when you were young?" I asked, searching his face.

"Even when I was young."

I breathed a sigh of relief.

Choco Joe shook his head and said, "What I am is a man with a teeny bit more perspective on things than you or Mr. K or anyone at this studio. And it seems that I'm the only one who sees that no matter how great your excellency may seem, he's only human. He's capable of making mistakes just like you or me."

I glared at him and said, "Take that back."

"Take what back?"

"His Excellency's the most honorable man in our country. You've no right to say anything bad about Him. Absolutely no right."

He chuckled. "You really ought to listen to yourself, kid. You'd get a kick out of it."

"You don't understand because you're a stupid American. You want our country to be poor and backward forever. That way we'll always have to turn to your country for chewing gum and toothpaste. You can't stomach the idea that some day soon we're going to be richer and more powerful than your country."

"That's nonsense and you know it."

"It's not nonsense. It's the truth and you don't want to admit it. You can't accept the fact that we'll soon have a bullet train, and you still think of our country as a backward place with thatch houses and toothless women."

"I do not."

"You do too. That's why you don't support His Excellency. He's working to make our country strong and rich, and you can't stand that."

"You're a piece of work, kid." He shook his head and lit another cigarette.

"What's that mean? A piece of work?" It was an English idiom I hadn't yet learned.

"Figure it out, kid. You're a genius, ain't you?"

My lips tightened, and my head began to shake. I could feel heat rising up my face. Then I exploded. "I don't have to listen to you! You're a spy!"

Choco Joe turned to me slowly and said, "What did you say?"

"You're a spy! You're a CIA operative posing as an entertainer! You're here to make sure we don't say anything bad about the U.S.A."

"I'll pretend I didn't hear that, kid."

"I'm not afraid of you. I'm not afraid of you or the CIA. Even if your agents kidnapped me and killed me, I wouldn't care. It'd be an honor to die for my country."

Choco Joe lunged at me, grabbed me by my arms, and shook me violently. His fingers dug into my skin, and his eyes bulged out of their sockets. "There's no honor in dying for any country. You hear me? No honor whatsoever!"

I didn't say anything.

Choco Joe let go of me and shrank away. With his head turned away, he said, "Sorry, kid. I didn't mean to get so worked up. Forget everything I said, okay?"

My arms throbbed. Even without looking, I knew that there would soon be dark bruises where Choco Joe had grabbed me.

The door swung open and Mr. K rushed inside. "Break's over, guys. Let's get back to work."

I started walking toward the door. Choco Joe shouted after me, "Hey, kid!"

I turned around slowly.

Choco Joe smiled sheepishly and gently tossed a pack of Lucky Strikes toward me. I caught it as if it were an easy infield fly.

"Keep it," he said. "A peace offering."

Mr. K stared at me and Choco Joe with a confused expression on his face. I put the pack in my pocket and walked out into the hall.

CHAPTER 7
The United Revolutionary Party

Winter melted away and the Rose of Sharon, our national flower, bloomed seemingly overnight on the hillsides all around the capital, adding a bright purple accent to the landscape. Yet another tunnel dug by the North Korean Army in an attempt to invade our country was discovered near the DMZ, sounding an alarm to all those who foolishly believed that reunification with North Korea should be achieved at any cost.

Editorials in *Korea Tomorrow* decried the declining mores that drove hemlines above women's knees, and thousands of school children celebrated the season with pilgrimages to His Excellency's hometown in North Kyoungsang Province.

I was planning my own pilgrimage when H-I-J appeared once again at KBS and escorted me back to the Blue House. On the way, we passed the same construction site along the Han. The building was finished now, and across its side hung a large white banner that read, "Beware of Communists at Work and at Home."

Minutes later, I was back in the room with the bamboo door. His Excellency sighed and said, "Do you know the story of the lonely spinster who fell victim to a North Korean spy who pretended to love her?"

"No, Your Excellency," I said.

"She was a school teacher at a prestigious high school for girls here in Seoul. She was described in one of her yearly reviews as an exemplary teacher, if somewhat quiet and reserved. She was originally from Pusan, and I suspect that she must have been lonely in this city. It's not clear how she met him. But he wooed her with skill. It's easy to imagine how he must have approached her. Such seemingly chance meetings take place hundreds of times in a city like ours. Inebriated by the attention of a handsome young man, she soon did everything he wanted of her. She gave him money and let him turn her apartment into a safe house for other subversives. Within a year, he'd turned her into an opium addict and forced her to sell her body. Of course, all proceeds went to support terrorism and subversion. In the end, driven by torment and desperation, she ended it all by jumping out her window. The spy who drove her to suicide was later apprehended and dealt with, but there's nothing we can do to bring the quiet school teacher back. You see, Boy Genius. Even as you and I sit here and talk, communists are ruining the lives of our trusting citizens."

"I didn't know, Your Excellency."

He nodded gently and clapped His hands. Immediately three bodyguards rushed inside carrying large boxes of magazines, books, and film reels.

As the boxes piled up around me, His Excellency said, "It has been one of my many lifelong goals that our democratic society be cleansed of communist contamination. The communists have done enough to disrupt life as we once knew it. Families have been separated, and brothers have had to turn their guns on one another. Communism is a goiter that cannot be allowed to spread. It must be wiped out from our midst once and for all. I beg you to go through these publications to make sure none have been contaminated by unhealthy ideas."

"It is as good as done, Your Excellency."

He smiled and tousled my hair playfully. "I knew I could count on you, Boy Genius."

For the next two weeks, I parked myself on top of a pile of comic books and began examining the cultural artifacts before me. Most of the books espoused ideas that were harmless. Ninety-nine percent of the stories that reached children were rehashed plots lifted from old American movies and Japanese comic books. But the remaining one percent wasn't as innocent.

It was clear that a popular children's cartoon about a little league baseball team that travels to Guam was really a disguised barb poking fun at His Excellency's upcoming summit with a prominent West African statesman. It was also clear that a popular film directed by a former college professor about a wayward prince from the thirteenth century was a carefully disguised critique of His Excellency's New Village Campaign. As such, they could only have been created by communists who were acting under direct orders of the PRK Army and its bastard child, the United Revolutionary Party, an outlawed underground organization that spread chaos through acts of urban terrorism and sabotage. I rejoiced in my role in fighting the URP because they had set the blaze at the National Theater that took my aunt's life two years before my birth.

After I made my report, His Excellency stared at me for a long while, then said, "You've done well, Boy Genius. I think it's time we had a drink."

I didn't dare tell Him that Father's father had drunk himself to death or that Mother had begged me and made me promise that I'd never touch alcohol. To bring up such trifles in the face of an international statesman seemed somehow inappropriate.

His Excellency opened a drawer and took out a bottle of soju and two shot glasses. He set the glasses on the desk and poured me a drink. I returned the favor and poured Him a drink. Then, His Excellency held up His glass and said, "To our Motherland. May she prosper and regain the glory of her long and majestic past!"

We clinked glasses and drank. The liquor burned my throat and instantly warmed my cheeks. His Excellency laughed heartily and poured me another drink. As I downed the second glass, I laughed inwardly at Mother's needless worries.

As if sensing my thoughts, His Excellency said, "Be good to your parents, Boy Genius. They may not always seem right, but they always have good intentions. As you grow older, you'll see that they're not the idiots you believe them to be."

"Yes, Your Excellency."

He leaned back in His chair and propped His feet up on His desk. It was the most casual pose I'd ever seen Him in. "I wish Chi-Man were more like you, Boy Genius."

I remained silent.

"Do you know he cursed me the other night? I reprimanded him for getting a D in his calligraphy class. A mild scolding. I hardly raised my voice and I didn't lay a hand on him. I've never laid a hand on him. I don't believe that such a show of force can truly persuade anyone, especially not a child. Still, Chi-Man stormed out of the room muttering curses under his breath. He called me a loser and a has-been. He didn't think I heard him, but I did. My own son."

"I'm sorry, Your Excellency."

"There's no need to apologize. It's not your fault. If anyone's to blame, it's myself. I didn't spend nearly enough time with the boy when he was young. He and I never got to sit together like this and share a drink. I imagine you and your father must spend much time together, Boy Genius."

"No, Your Excellency. My father hardly spends any time with me."

"I'm sorry, Boy Genius." His Excellency was quiet for a while, then said, "Do you know what the worst thing in the world is?"

I thought for a moment, then said, "Is it communism, Your Excellency?"

"A good answer, most worthy of your genius. Communism is wholly foreign to our nation. It turns diligent men lazy and slowly robs even the most compassionate of their humanity. It is immoral and demonstrates no respect to the creator or our ancestors. In a word, it is outright un-Korean. But there is something even worse than communism."

"What could possibly be worse than communism, Your Excellency?"

He smiled. "Breaking a promise, Boy Genius. Breaking one's word. This is far worse. Before nationalities, before political or religious beliefs, and even before kinship, keeping one's word is what makes us human. It's the only thing that binds one person to the next. Without it, we are no better than animals, no better than wild dogs. Take my bodyguards, for example, the men who guard the gates of this palace and escort you through its numerous corridors. They are the elite of the army, the best soldiers in the entire country. I selected them from the troops myself. Some in my cabinet criticize me for placing too much faith in the military, but I cannot help it. I trust soldiers. It was they who fought off the North Korean commandoes who made an attempt on my life many years ago, long before you were born. Surely you know of the incident?"

He paused as if He were waiting for an answer. I nodded. "I've read about the incident, Your Excellency."

"Good, good. This is what's so nice about talking to a genius. One doesn't have the burden of having to fill in the dreadful details of any story. We can communicate in shorthand." He guffawed.

His laugh was infectious, and I couldn't help but laugh as well.

He continued, "I will never forget that night. The North Korean commandoes had disguised themselves as a group of Japanese tourists, but my men were not easily fooled. They were apprehended at the Blue House Gate."

I already knew that much from the newspaper.

His Excellency continued, "You may have guessed already, but H-I-J, the man who ferries you here from the television studio, is the soldier who saved my life that night. He was the first to spot the North Korean commandoes at the Blue House gate and the first to fight them off. In the end, he killed them all, but one managed to squirt acid on his face. That's how he got that scar. Some find the scar to be hideous, but to me, his scar is a badge of his patriotism and his hatred of communism, North Korean aggression, and Soviet imperialism. When I asked him later why he had done what he did, he said, 'I made a promise to protect you.' He'd made a promise to protect me. I ask you, Boy Genius, can there be a more profound or elegant response than that? That's what makes him human and heroic. You must always keep your word. If you do not, you're no better than a wild dog. Do you understand, Boy Genius?"

"Yes, Your Excellency. I understand."

"Good." He smiled and poured me another drink. I drank it down in one gulp, not minding one bit that my own father had never sat down and drank with me.

CHAPTER 8
New Village

That summer, during a break while taping a special to commemorate His Excellency's courageous takeover of power, which deposed the old regime and returned order to our nation, Mr. K rushed in frantically to the storage room where Choco Joe and I were engaged in a fierce game of Chinese chess. As usual, Choco Joe had lined up his pawns in front of his king in what he called his "Great Wall of China stratagem." In contrast, I had pushed my pawns forward in an all-out blitzkrieg attack, which I called my "Operation Rolling Thunder."

"Have you heard the news, Boy Genius?" Mr. K said, struggling to catch his breath.

"What news?" I asked, looking up from the board.

Mr. K took out a handkerchief from the breast pocket of his linen jacket and dabbed it lightly against his shiny forehead. "Our Virtuous First Lady has been gunned down and killed by an assassin at the National Theater. His Excellency was making a speech when it happened. The news just came over the wire."

I was speechless.

Choco Joe put a hand on my shoulder and said, "I'm sorry, kid."

For several seconds, I couldn't say anything. Finally, I managed to stammer, "But she's a saint."

Mr. K sighed and shut his eyes.

"Why would anyone do such a thing?" I asked.

"I'm sorry, kid," Choco Joe repeated.

"They haven't released the details. We'll learn more in the days to come," said Mr. K. He turned to Choco Joe and held up two fingers in front of his mouth as if he were smoking an imaginary cigarette.

"But you've quit for six years, Mr. K," said Choco Joe.

"Please, Choco Joe."

Choco Joe nodded sympathetically and handed him a cigarette. He then turned to me and offered me one too. I took it and headed for the door.

"Where are you going, Boy Genius?" Choco Joe shouted after me.

"I have to go see Him," I said, then trudged out the door. As I walked down the long hallway, the First Lady's beautiful face popped into my head and I thought back to New Year's Eve when she'd welcomed me so graciously to her home. It pained me that I would never see Her beautiful smile again and that His Excellency's three children would now have to grow up without a mother.

Outside, I hailed a taxi to the Blue House. The cabbie, a rough-looking sort with a five o'clock shadow, who appeared on the surface not to have a single ounce of sensitivity or intelligence, said, "His Excellency should send commandoes to the North. Have them take out the head commie's son. Give those red bastards a taste of their own medicine." He then sucked in smoke from his cigarette with a kind of desperation that moved me. Like everyone else, he was mourning a terrible loss.

As we raced along the Han, plaintive cries swirled all around us. People were gathered in small clusters everywhere, at bus stops, noodle shops, and newsstands, crying and doing their best to console one another. Strangely, the sight of this impromptu mobilization was comforting. I was reminded yet again of His Excellency's infinite wisdom. Despite being strangers, we were all, indeed, cousins.

The sentries at the Blue House gate waved my cab through without hesitation, thus signaling that I was now a recognized member of His Excellency's inner circle. Outside the front steps of the Blue House, the cabbie got out with me to salute the flag, which was flying at half-mast.

The cab disappeared back out through the gate, and I entered the Blue House. The Hall of Patriots was completely empty, and it seemed to me as if three decades had passed since the New Year's Eve Gala where I had first met His Excellency and the First Family. I made my way down the steps to the basement corridor and continued on to His Excellency's study. Then, just as I was about to knock on the bamboo door, a hand grabbed my shoulder and yanked me back forcefully.

It was H-I-J. He shook his head and said, "I'm sorry, Boy Genius. But you can't go in there right now."

"But I have to see Him."

"His Excellency has left strict orders."

"But I want to console Him."

He leaned down to me and put both hands firmly on my shoulders. "We all do, Boy Genius. But His Excellency instructed us that He is not to be disturbed. Not by His children. Not by anyone. Not even you, Boy Genius."

"But . . ."

"Try to understand, Boy Genius. His Excellency has just lost His wife. I know you're just a boy, but you must have an inkling of how terrible that is."

"I'm not just a boy."

"Come back in three days, Boy Genius. You'll be able to see Him then. I give you my word."

I trudged back down the long dark corridor. My footsteps were heavy. I was disappointed and sad, but deep inside, I understood His Excellency's need to be alone. He was, after all, a great man of history.

CHAPTER 9
Kant and Descartes

Three days later, the headline on the front page of *Korea Today* read, "NORTH KOREAN ASSASSIN COMMITS SUICIDE." Next to the article was a photograph, the kind often found on college I.D. cards, of a sickly young man who looked as if he'd never seen sunshine in his entire life. The blank expression on his face revealed nothing except that he was twisted to the core. The article described him as an elite North Korean commando who had masqueraded the past four years as a philosophy student at Yonsei University. In a separate article, the student's landlady, a middle-aged woman of below-average I.Q., claimed ignorance and insisted that she was just as shocked as everyone else to learn that her tenant had been a PRK agent. An accompanying editorial called for a thorough investigation of the philosophy department and all who had come in contact with the murderous scoundrel.

In deference to the First Lady's passing, the roads in the capital were closed to motor traffic and private businesses were shut down for the day. Since there were no taxis, I started biking to the Blue House on a blue Schwinn that had been a gift from one of *The Boy Genius Hour's* many sponsors. I was very proud of the fact that I'd learned to ride it in twenty minutes to the amazement of the two interns—both recent graduates of Seoul University—whom Mr. K had assigned to teach me.

The streets were empty and silent as if the city had been evacuated. But outside every door there was a flag flying at half-mast. I couldn't stop and salute every flag, but I made sure to think patriotic thoughts as I raced past. According to the Great Kon-Fu-Tze, an honorable subject had to mourn the loss of his ruler for three years. The same period of mourning was required of children for their parents.

At the Blue House gate, the same sentry from three days earlier stopped me and said, "You cannot go inside."

My first reaction was that the guard was teasing me. I stared at him for a moment then started to continue through the gate. Immediately, he lowered his rifle and blocked my path.

"You cannot go inside."

"But I'm here to see His Excellency. His Excellency is expecting me."

"You cannot go inside."

"But you waved me through just the other day," I said, motioning toward the Blue House.

"You cannot go inside."

"But H-I-J told me to come back. It's been three days now."

"You cannot go inside."

A large German sedan pulled up next to the gate. It was the same car that had ferried H-I-J and me along the Han on numerous occasions. Immediately, the sentries stood at attention and saluted. I rushed over and tapped on the rear passenger window. The window slid down slowly, and H-I-J leaned his head out. "What seems to be the problem here?" he asked.

I pointed to the guards and said, "They won't let me through, H-I-J. Please explain to them that I'm here to see His Excellency."

H-I-J nodded sympathetically and said, "Don't worry about a thing, Boy Genius. There's been some confusion here, but I'll take care of everything."

He then turned to the sentries and shouted, "Shoot this boy if he ever shows up here again!"

The sentries saluted, and the sedan pulled away into the compound. I stood agape and stared after the car in a daze, completely baffled by the strange turn of events.

The sentry shoved me with the end of his rifle and steered me away from the compound. I turned my bike around and coasted down the hill. The sun hung bright directly overhead. All around me, a heavy cloud of spores floated about in the gentle summer breeze, and the trees that lined the road seemed sinister and sick, their branches more crooked and twisted than ever. Something was terribly amiss and I needed desperately to see a friendly face.

Before I got twenty feet inside the KBS lobby, Choco Joe ran up to me frantically and said, "I'm sorry, Boy Genius, but you have to go home."

"What's going on, Choco Joe?"

"I haven't the time to explain. But you have to trust me on this one."

"But we haven't taped tonight's episode," I said.

"There isn't going to be an episode tonight."

"What?"

"Look, Boy Genius. I can't make heads or tails of it, but things have changed here. Some people came to talk to Mr. K earlier today. He ordered me not to talk to you, but I couldn't leave you hanging like that."

"I don't understand."

"Neither do I, Boy Genius. Neither do I." He sighed and shook his head.

There were footsteps, then Mr. K appeared at the end of the corridor with two security guards flanked at his side. Their footsteps quickly drowned out all other sound. As soon as they reached us, Mr. K yanked Choco Joe away, then turned to the guards. "This boy is trespassing."

"Mr. K," I said.

He didn't say anything. He just stood there with his arms across his chest while the two security guards carried me to the exit. As they pushed me through the revolving door, Choco Joe shouted, "I'll write you! And I'll send you some oranges!"

The two guards carried me outside and deposited me in the parking lot. Several hours later, when it was dark, I retrieved my bicycle from the bike rack and started for home.

The streets were still quiet and empty. The air didn't smell of alcohol, and there were no stumbling drunks or raucous laughter. As I passed a shabby noodle stand, the proprietor slapped the empty wooden bench in front of him that should have been filled with patrons and muttered, "Dogshit!"

No day laborers or other members of the uneducated underclass were drinking their paychecks away. As the merchant's grumbling echoed behind me, the realization set in that something terrible had happened. I'd never been turned away from anywhere since becoming a genius. Now, the only place I was welcome was home.

CHAPTER 10

Area of a Circle = πr^2

Mother and Father were sitting in front of the TV when I got home.

"The strangest thing happened to me today," I said.

"It's been a strange day for us too," said Mother. She looked more tired than I ever remembered her being.

I sat down next to them and said, "I'm hoping things will right themselves tomorrow."

They nodded listlessly and turned back to the TV, a twenty-one-inch Sony that had been a gift from Samsung, another of *The Boy Genius Hour*'s many sponsors. The familiar KBS logo was on the screen. Choco Joe appeared in his usual boxing outfit accompanied by the show's cheerful theme music, a simple melody played on the harmonica. He then swung his fists in a flurry of combinations, connecting straights to hooks and uppercuts as if he were warming up for a title fight in a Third World jungle. It was his usual entrance. Some seconds later, he saluted and sang, *"He can fight back commies with his brain. He can add faster than a speeding train. He's a whiz in baduk and chess. His picture's there in Guinness. He's the smartest ever born. So eat your spinach and eat your corn."*

Then, Choco Joe jumped up in the air and shouted, "Say hello to Lucky Chang, the smartest boy in the world!"

There was canned applause, and out waddled a pudgy boy wearing a sparkling white taekwondo uniform. The boy's face was a perfect circle, his hair was gleaming and parted in the middle, and his eyes were just tiny slits like a Chinaman's. He waved his hands stupidly and stammered, in a frail girlish voice, "L-L-Long live K-K-Korea. L-L-Long l-l-live His Excellency the M-M-Most Honorable P-P-President Park!"

Mother stared at me blankly for a long while, then pulled me to her bosom. "I'm so sorry, Boy Genius."

"But he's a stutterer. Why would they replace me with a stutterer?"

"I don't know, Boy Genius. I don't know," said Mother, stroking the back of my head.

From outside our courtyard, a passing street peddler yelled, "Fresh tofu here! Fresh tofu!"

His voice sounded strangely melodic as if he were singing an ancient dirge.

Father turned off the TV and muttered, "Damn tofu sellers." Then he stormed outside.

For the rest of the evening, I lay quietly in Mother's arms and breathed in her familiar and soothing fragrance. As always, she smelled of dried seaweed.

CHAPTER 11

Lucky Chang's Seven T-t-t-tell-t-t-tale S-s-s-signs of C-c-c-commie B-b-bastards:

1) C-c-c-commie b-b-bastards act nervous and don't know common things that even children know l-l-like prices of candy bars and names of streets.

2) C-c-c-commie b-b-bastards stay up late at night to communicate with other c-c-c-commie b-b-bastards via transmitter radios. Be on the lookout for radio sounds and static late at night.

3) C-c-c-commie b-b-bastards snatch purses, pick pockets, and burglarize homes in order to frighten hard-working citizens.

4) C-c-c-commie b-b-bastards read c-c-c-commie b-b-bastard books and leaflets and try to get others to read them too. Turn c-c-c-commie b-b-bastard propaganda into your teachers or police as soon as you find them.

5) C-c-c-commie b-b-bastards complain about their wages and go strike. They make demonstrations instead of working hard.

6) C-c-c-commie b-b-bastards don't study hard and they don't listen to their parents and they talk back to their teachers.

7) C-c-c-commie b-b-bastards drain the country by having more than two children. Two for patriots. More for c-c-c-commie b-b-bastards.

Long live the Republic! Long l-l-live His Excellency the Most Honorable President Park! Catch a c-c-c-commie b-b-bastard and win a h-h-house.

CHAPTER 12

$2 = 1$

My sudden fall from grace made no headlines. It didn't even get a mention in the back page of the hundreds of third-rate tabloids that snot-nosed orphans hawked on street corners and at bus stops. The New Village Campaign continued as usual, His Excellency announced His latest five-year plan, and a nation of so-called cousins went about their lives as if its youngest national treasure had never meant anything to them.

My only consolation came from a box of oranges that appeared at our doorstep a week after my dismissal from KBS. The oranges were of the best quality, fresh from Cheju, a remote island off the southernmost tip of the peninsula. It was a small gesture, but I was grateful for Choco Joe's kindness.

Meanwhile, Mother was ousted from her teaching post at Virtuous First Lady Middle School for Girls and Father was dismissed from his job at His Excellency's Central Post Office. No explanations were ever given. Besides the lost income, my parents were wounded deeply by the fact that not one student or co-worker visited them in the aftermath of their dismissals to inquire about their well-being. Like me, they too had become lepers in a land of purported cousins.

Cut off from money and friends, my family was forced to move out of our spacious two-story house across the street from His Excellency Memorial University to a succession of smaller and increasingly decrepit homes, further and further removed from the center of the capital. Father attempted a number of harebrained schemes to earn some money, but nothing could stave off the inevitable. In just six months, we ended up in a dark six-foot-by-six-foot aluminum box that sat on the worst plot in a village of make-shift shanties fashioned out of cardboard boxes and Coca-Cola bottles. Mother blamed everything on her fate. Father kept muttering, "It's this damn country."

Our new neighbors, mostly itinerant tofu peddlers and rag pickers, all feeble-minded former peasants who had drifted to the capital from the countryside, took no pity on us. Instead, they guffawed and shouted through rotting black gums, as they punctuated their speech by spitting dark liquids at their feet: "Don't worry about a thing. If all three of you learn to beg well and peddle chewing gum on the street, you may get back a tenth of what you lost in nine hundred years!"

Their rustic ways terrified us, especially Mother, who had spent her whole life in the capital. Not an hour went by when she didn't take me aside and say, "Be careful of the neighbors, especially old rag pickers with beards. They abduct boys your age and sell them as slaves on shrimp boats."

Despite Mother's entreaties, I couldn't sit at home and stare at the walls. Articles in the old issues of *Korea Tomorrow* with which the walls were papered were painful reminders of my former life. Moreover, Mother's increasingly haggard appearance was a silent accusation that I was somehow to blame for our demise. It was I who had lifted our family out of our ordinary existence, so it must also have been I who had piloted us to the lap of misery. Had I been able to smoke during this time, I might have fared better, but Lucky Strikes were now a luxury from the past. A pack of Lucky Strikes at the East Gate Black Market cost more than the price of three bowls of Chinese noodles.

Wanting to forget the sudden and inexplicable downfall that had beset my family, I sought solace in the mindless games of the shantytown children: landmine, played with flattened bottle-caps on hastily-drawn grids; and bomb shelter, played with mud bombs and broken bottles. In addition, we caught dragonflies and tied string leashes to their backs. And we yanked the tails off of rats simply because we could. In no time, I became just another street urchin, indistinguishable from the thousands of soot-covered monsters who swarmed the city hawking newspapers, nail clippers, and chewing gum.

This second childhood didn't last long, however. When I returned home one afternoon and proudly held up a plastic bag holding my day's haul of 38 shiny green flies, Mother collapsed on our dirt floor, pounded the earth with her palms, and wailed, "What good is I.Q.? What good is genius?"

I was taken aback by her sudden outburst. Never in all my years had I seen a single tear fall from her eyes. She'd remained impassive when her youngest sister died trying to escape the fire that gutted the National Theater, and again when her mother succumbed to lung cancer after living next to a Samsung petrochemical plant for 38 years. Yet here she was crying for me, her only son who had once been a national treasure but now amused himself by hunting flies with a plastic bag. I couldn't bear to see her like that. She was a strong and proud woman, who had given up a scholarship that would have allowed her to study abroad to make a name for herself as a woman of letters so that she could marry, stay close to her father, cook, clean, give birth to a son, and fulfill her role as a dutiful Korean daughter. More than anyone, she knew what it meant to have to live a life that didn't belong to her.

Left with no hope, I turned to the only man in the peninsula capable of righting wrongs.

3/8/19XX
Boy Genius
Star Village Apartments

His Excellency the Most Honorable President Park
c/o The Blue House

Your Excellency the Most Honorable President Park:
Long live the Republic! Long live Your Excellency the Most Honorable President Park!

I turn to Your Excellency for You are my last hope. After being removed from our posts without explanation, my family and I have suffered both materially and spiritually. We lack those basic materials necessary for survival. More importantly, we are no longer able to use our skills for the good of the nation. The latter has been devastating.

I seek no favor or preference on this matter but plead only that my parents and I be allowed to once again work for the country we love. I appeal to Your Excellency not as a boy genius or a former servant, but as one whose humble grandfather lived in the village next to Your own in North Kyungsang Province, the true heartland of Korea.

I know full well how presumptuous I am being in making this plea, but I appeal to Your Excellency's compassion and infinite wisdom and take this risk solely because of my concern for our nation. I put my life in Your Excellency's most noble and generous hands, and remain as always,

Your humble boy genius,
Boy Genius

CHAPTER 13

Queen Min and the Ninja

It was near the end of summer at the height of the rainy season. A typical monsoon day from Manila had been transported magically to the streets of our shantytown. Thick rain spilled down in fierce rat-a-tat machine gun bursts, and three battalions of giant black rats with thick quill-like fur scrambled for cover like a column of Mao Tse Tung guerillas. Black water, the consistency of rancid soy milk, covered the streets, and loose garbage floated about like sampans adrift near harbor.

The monsoons brought more rain than in any previous year. Bridges, roads, and entire villages were swept away to the sea, and thousands of displaced peasants from the countryside trudged reluctantly to the capital with only the slim hope of finding work at the newest government-subsidized textile factory. Religious zealots of all persuasions, led by charismatic bald men who claimed to talk directly with a hundred different deities, gathered on top of Mount Nam and held frenzied tent revivals. All prayed for the rain to sweep over the city and strike down sinners the way it had once done in biblical times.

I sat on the stoop outside my shanty and listened to the rain. The urchins had stopped bothering to come around looking for me. I was tired of them. I had been a star of my own TV show. A handful of them would grow up to deliver Chinese food if they were lucky and ambitious. The rest would grow up to haul dirt from one corner of the earth to another, the way their forefathers had done for thousands of years.

As he did every three days, the mailman appeared at our village on a rickety bicycle. He had on an ancient green poncho held together by duct tape, and cheap strips of blue vinyl were wrapped around his legs to keep them protected from the mud that splattered up from the ground.

I rushed up to him and said, "Anything?"

He touched the brim of his regulation cap, and then handed me the following telegram:

> BG: Long live His Excellency-STOP-His Excellency instructed me to send you this-STOP-Have you seen Lucky Chang Show?-STOP-It's terrific!-STOP-No jobs except cram-school instructor in Cheju-STOP-Come see me at InvaCom—HIJ

I read the telegram four times to make sure I hadn't misread anything. But nothing I did could change the fact that His Excellency hadn't even deigned to respond to me personally. Instead, he'd had H-I-J, a goon whose sole worth lay in the fact that he'd killed twelve North Koreans, tell me that the only place for my genius was a fourth-rate cram school on an island of ignorant fishermen whose children all had below-average I.Q.s. I tore the telegram into a hundred pieces and let them fall to the puddle on the ground.

While I struggled to contain my rage, the mailman said, "Being a cram-school instructor's not so bad, Boy Genius. And Cheju's not that remote. You might even get to like the scenery there. The rocks there are magnificent."

I glared at him. His eyes were exactly six centimeters apart, his lips were of average thickness, and his nose was fleshy and red like a ripe strawberry. It was clear that he'd gotten his job through nepotism and would always be extremely content to ride his second-hand bicycle to deliver twaddle to illiterate peasants.

"Your uncle should be shot for getting you this job!" I shouted.

"I didn't mean . . ."

"You stole this job from someone more capable and smart than you. Because of you, someone more capable is starving!"

Without a word, the mailman backed away nervously, got on his bicycle, and disappeared down the hill.

I returned to my stoop and stared at the large puddle in front of me. Tiny remains of the telegram bobbed just above the surface and seemed to mock me.

I turned to the sky and screamed at the top of my lungs, "Your Excellency, Your Excellency, why have You forsaken me?"

There was no answer. Just the sound of the rain. From the shack next door, a baby began crying. I hoped it had a below-average I.Q.

CHAPTER 14
Gold Mountain

The following morning, I sat my parents down on our dirt floor and said, "Our time in Korea has come to an end. We've no choice but to leave for a bigger and better place."

Mother glanced nervously at me and then at Father. "But my father and sisters are all here. And this has been our home for 5,000 years."

I shook my head firmly. "Everything's been decided. The only thing left for you to do is to pack our meager possessions. I'll take care of everything else."

"Please, Boy Genius," she said. "Think this over carefully. I know things are bad here, but there's no guarantee that they will be better someplace else. As bad as things are, we have family here. We were born Korean and we'll die Korean. This is our home."

"Enough!" I shouted.

"But . . ."

"The decision's been made. There's nothing left to discuss now."

Mother glanced nervously at Father. "How can we let a boy make such a decision?"

He sighed and said, "Let him handle it. He's smarter than the both of us."

Mother lowered her eyes and said no more.

I stood up and said, "Good. Everything's settled. I'll go make the arrangements."

I rushed straight to the headquarters of the Central Invasion Committee, an arm of the KCIA. Their office was located in a nondescript gray building in Inchon next to the statue of General Douglas MacArthur, for which penniless French children had never contributed a dime. A long line of people with umbrellas were already huddled along the tall iron gate. I joined them and waited. Every now and then, the woman in front of me, who reeked of soy sauce, stomped her feet and muttered, "Damn sons of bitches."

The wait was long and unbearable. It was wet and cold. Moreover, not one person came up to me to ask for an autograph. His Excellency had succeeded in completely erasing me from the collective consciousness.

Just before dusk, I was let inside and taken to a small windowless room in the cellar.

H-I-J's familiar face greeted me with a warm smile. "So it's come to this. The Great Boy Genius wishes to leave his homeland."

"Please don't make this any harder than it needs to be," I said.

"I wouldn't dream of such a thing. You may not believe it, Boy Genius, but I'm genuinely glad to see you."

I said nothing.

"Well, I can see by your face that the feeling's not mutual. But I do hope that you'll appreciate the kindness I'm bestowing on you by granting you this exit interview. Anyway, why don't you sit."

I sat down on a small metal stool. Directly above me, a light bulb that had been calibrated to shine only on me burned brightly. As I stared at this bulb, H-I-J began pacing slowly in front of me. "We do not mind you leaving, Boy Genius. We expected it and we think it is for the best. Frankly, we're surprised it didn't happen earlier. However, that being so, it is of the utmost importance that certain arrangements be made for your own good and that of certain nameless individuals. Please bear in mind that all this is being done because of your good standing with a certain most honorable individual. Were it not for the intervention of this great nameless being, whose honor and generosity knows no bounds, you would not have been granted this meeting and you surely would have continued to rot in your utter insignificance.

But measures have been taken to grant you mercy. In your own small way, you too have helped to crush Soviet imperialism and North Korean aggression."

I said nothing. I just stared at H-I-J's scar and took in just how indescribably ugly he really was. His scar, which would have devastated most faces, actually improved his appearance by deflecting attention away from his crooked nose and three rows of teeth. Somehow, it seemed fitting that a person with H-I-J's job would be as ugly as he was, and I couldn't help but smile.

H-I-J leaned his face angrily in front of mine and shouted, "Why are you smiling? What part of Soviet imperialism and North Korean aggression do you find so irrepressibly amusing?"

"Nothing. Nothing at all."

He took a deep breath and collected himself. "You should know that we're being extremely generous with you. Many have suffered far greater for far less. But you already know this and I have said far too much."

"I still don't know what I did wrong."

"Enough!" he shouted. "You're not here to plead your case. The time for explanations is over. Everything has been arranged. It's time for you to start a new life." He thrust a stack of forms before me and slapped the top page. "These documents will prove that your perspective never existed. You never met with His Excellency the Most Honorable President Park or me or anyone related to our noble democratic republic that upholds the uncontestable merits of democracy, human rights, anti-communism, and free enterprise. You know nothing about the abduction of parliamentarians who have never disappeared or the alleged disappearance of other commie bastards and North Korean stooges who have disturbed our peace and threatened our stability. Nor do you know anything about the arrangements which we have not made with certain representatives of foreign nations and business leaders who do not exist. In short, you have heard nothing. You have seen nothing. And you have known nothing. Of course, it follows that you will speak nothing and you will betray nothing. Do you understand what I have not said and what you have not heard in this room that does not exist?"

"I understand." I signed the forms that did not exist which H-I-J never thrust before me under a dim bulb that never shone on anyone at all.

CHAPTER 15

$nC_{r-1}\ xn-r+1\ yr-1$

Mother's father, four sisters, and a dozen other members of her clan saw us off at Kimpo International on a sunny autumn morning. Unlike Mother and Lucky Chang, whose faces were perfect circles with a radius of 9.5 centimeters, Mother's four sisters' faces were classic ovals. Despite their beauty, each knew she had disappointed from the first breath a family cursed with no sons. While my six cousins, all snot-nosed urchins with below-average I.Q.s who had never ridden on an airplane, looked on with envy, each aunt hugged me, pressed a hard-boiled egg into my hand for the journey across the ocean, and told me to be a good boy.

Across from me, Father stood by himself, holding two knapsacks which contained all of our earthly possessions. As always, he seemed to be uncomfortable around Mother's family. I didn't blame him. Though I didn't know the full details, it was obvious that they had disapproved of Mother marrying him. Like the thousands of displaced peasants with bad teeth who'd drifted to the capital after the war, Father had been a penniless young man with no prospects for a stable future when his path crossed Mother's.

No one had come to see Father off. The only remaining member of his clan, a hunchbacked older sister, was too sick to make the ten-hour trip to the capital from Bonghwa, the remote village of his birth where stubborn commie bastards still waged guerilla war from the mountains. I doubted she would have come even if she were able. She hated the city and loathed my father for leaving her and Bonghwa. The only time I saw her, she'd told me in a hoarse voice tinged with the rabid excitement of hermits and shamans, "The city is an evil place. Before your father ventured to the city he was a handsome young man filled with energy and bright thoughts. Now, he doesn't even return to pay his respect to the memory of our father."

Mother was standing with her father, a wizened, toothless old man whose curved spine made him look like a walking question mark. He clung desperately to Mother's arms and said, "You will never return and I will die without ever seeing you again."

Mother wiped tears away from her eyes and sighed, "We will be fine, Father. It will be difficult at first, but we will persevere. Then we will come back to see you with a sack filled with gold coins and dollar bills. We'll bring back washing machines for all of Boy Genius's aunts. And we'll make sure to send you gift packages at all the holidays filled with chocolates, Tang, and blue jeans."

The old man just shook his head and clung to her even more desperately. "Lies. All lies. None of these things will ever come true. You and your husband will die in a foreign land surrounded by strangers, and no one will even tend to your graves. All of you will die before I do, and I'll be left all alone with no one to take care of me!"

While everyone went over to try and calm the old man, Aunt Six, who had been trampled by two thousand screaming revelers fighting to escape fire and smoke, materialized before me in a pink hanbok matted with blood. She pressed no eggs in my palm. Instead, she slapped me hard across the face and whispered coldly in my ear, "No matter what happens, do not seek revenge. Do not wage war. Your parents have already lived through one war. They cannot survive another."

I said nothing, and I didn't tremble. Unlike my superstitious countrymen, I wasn't afraid of ghosts. Unable to stand the sight of my pathetic clan, I started walking toward the plane. Father followed me and Mother came soon behind. My aunts' loud cries boarded the plane with us.

Mother stared silently at the back of the seat in front of her, and Father muttered, "This damn country." I stared out the window at the matchbox houses below. I located our old two-story house and stared at it even after it disappeared under a cloud. Someone else was living there now, and a boy named Lucky Chang was living the life that should have been my own.

A perky young stewardess, whose bust-to-hip ratio met the rigorous standards set by Korean Airlines, filed down the aisle with a cart filled with soda pop. Smiling, she handed me a 7-Up and said, "What a cute boy."

I wanted to rip her throat out. Staring at her thick lipstick-stained mouth, I vowed to use my genius against His Excellency for as long as I lived.

BOOK II
The First Bogota War

CHAPTER 16
Bogota

My life as a genius in exile began in a ramshackle yellow-brick tenement owned by Mordechai Rubinstein, a third-generation Ukrainian Jew whose flair for irony had moved him to name the dwelling the King George Luxury Apartments. Located smack in the middle of Bogota, an insignificant fiefdom that reeked of urine and decay in the periphery of the Big Apple, the King George was built on top of what had once been the manure-laden pastures of German farmers whose American-born sons fought Hitler's krauts, Mussolini's wops, and Hirohito's nefarious yellow horde. Although it was no longer the heimat of patriotic descendants of European peasants, Bogota was still protected from the deadly rays of the First World sun by the tracks of the elevated 7-train, a child of mechanical ingenuity, which ferried the workers of the Third World to invisible jobs spit-shining the cracks and crevices of the city's most majestic skyscrapers.

Bogota's residents were made up of Third World detritus, the poor and disenfranchised who had made their way to the New World by traveling with nameless caravans from the world's most forgotten villages. Some had crossed oceans on makeshift rafts made of coconuts and burlap sacks. Others had obtained the necessary dog-eared documents from master forgers who passed on their ancient craft only to their firstborn. Still others had duped lonely Americans into marrying them with fleeting phrases recycled from old Hollywood movies. All had two things in common: their dirty brown skin smelled of sweat and strange spices, and their silent eyes held a thousand unspeakable secrets.

While Mother and Father searched desperately in Bogota's

three black markets for a way to turn what little youth they still had left into Kokkuho Enriched Rice and enough quarters to stave off Mordechai's monthly threats to throw us into the street, I sought to enlist in a North American branch of the many secret societies that had sprouted up in the Land of Morning Calm against His Excellency: the New Culture Study Society, Young Literary Writers' Society, Buddhist Youth Society, Donghak Society, Youth Association, Society for the Study of Nationalism, Christian Youth Economic Welfare Association, Kyongyu Society, and the Bachelors of Art Publication Society. But these groups had not yet made the journey across the Pacific, and the only subversive groups I found in Bogota were those made up of desperate brown men who met secretly in dank back rooms of corner bodegas, halal shops, and Chinese take-out dives. These meetings, in which disgruntled old men with beards breathed solidarity for Afghanistan and dreamed up a thousand and one secret plots to destroy Uncle Sam and blow up the Statue of Liberty, didn't interest me. I didn't care about workers, the proletariat, or the coming world jihad. All I wanted was to see His Excellency pay for the crimes he'd committed against me.

Frustrated and angry at my utter inability to put His Excellency before a firing squad, I roamed the streets aimlessly, simply to do something to mark the passing of time. It was then that I came upon a gang of a dozen children who were standing over an old man at the end of Bogota's darkest alley.

I crouched for cover behind a large green dumpster and looked on in secret. The urchins wore dirty rags thrown wildly over wiry limbs. Their hair was matted and long, and their skin was covered in soot and open sores.

A boy with wooly brown hair held up a small can of gasoline. Then, he calmly doused the old man with the clear liquid and lit him on fire.

The fire burned for a long while before the old man let out a horrific scream, jumped to his feet, and ran out of the alley. As he ran past me, the flames grew larger and a rush of heat warmed my face. I trembled slightly. It was the first time I'd ever seen a man burn like a piece of charcoal.

Suddenly, two boys grabbed me from behind and pushed me out into the open.

The boy who'd doused the old man moved toward me and shouted, "Who the hell are you? And what the hell are you doing spying on us?"

It was the tone of his voice more than anything else that provoked me. "I wasn't spying on you, you punk-ass bitch."

The other children turned silent and stared even more intently. The boy moved closer. He wasn't much bigger than me, but there was a menacing air about him. I knew immediately that he was their leader by the way the others followed him with eager anticipation.

The boy stopped just a foot away from me and stared at me for a long while. His left eye was brown, and the other was green. "You gotta learn to mind your own business in this town," he said.

"And you have to learn not to pick on strangers," I responded.

We stood facing each other for a little while longer. Then, before I realized it, the other children were gathered in a circle around us and chanting, "Fight! Fight! Fight!"

My opponent leaped high in the air, then lunged headfirst toward my stomach. I jumped aside and dodged what could easily have been a lethal blow. He bounced up and turned around in one smooth motion, then came at me again. I pivoted on my left foot and kicked him hard in the face with a crisp roundhouse. He fell to the ground, bounced up almost instantly, and lunged at me yet again as if my kick had had no effect whatsoever.

For the next three minutes, I gouged and bit and kicked and flailed. I used every move I'd learned from Choco Joe and drew upon all the rage that had built up inside me from His Excellency's betrayal. Despite all that, I was no match for the boy, who took my blows head-on and never seemed at all fazed by them.

In the end, I fell on my back and lay exhausted on the ground.

My chest heaved up and down. My lungs cried out for air. And all I could see was the dark sky above me.

The boy who had beat me peered at me from above. He didn't have a scratch on him. "I'm guessing you're new in town, so listen good. Mind your business and stay the hell away from here if you know what's good for you."

"Go to hell," I said, then spat my most venomous phlegm at him. The green glob flew toward him then, changed its mind, and landed straight on my nose.

The boy laughed and started to walk away.

I got up and shouted after him, "This isn't over! I'll be back tomorrow to kick your ass, you punk-ass bitch!"

He guffawed, then said, without ever turning around, which heaped even more insult to my pride, "Everyone says that, but no one ever does what they say."

I stared after him and the other wild children as they disappeared around the corner. Their scent, a unique blend of chlorine and oranges, lingered behind long after they were gone.

As I finally got up off the ground, the lid of the green dumpster swung open, and the tallest white man I'd ever seen crawled out slowly. He reeked of cheap booze. Large pits covered his face, and he had on a thick green army surplus jacket, despite the fact that it was nearly a hundred degrees out. Once he was out, he reached back inside and took out a small silver ukulele.

He tucked the instrument under his arm, then, without a word, trudged over to the far wall. There, he began peeing, moving slowly sideways as if he were a crab. When he was done, he farted loudly, and walked back toward me, pulling up his zipper. Behind him, a message had been written in urine, *"Viva Fidel. Viva la Revolucion."*

He came up to me and stared at me blankly for a long while. Then, he began strumming his ukulele rapidly with his large stubby fingers. The ensuing notes were surprisingly pleasant. Nodding his large box-like head rapidly in time to the music, he screeched at the top of his lungs, "Kung fu comes from China!

Do monks eat Aunt Ja-mima? Karate or kung fuey. Both can kill yo daddy!"

His voice sounded like two hundred hungry babies wailing in the middle of the night, and I couldn't help but cover my ears. When he finished his impromptu performance, he grinned as if he hadn't a worry in the world and said, "Name's Abraham Tomic and I'm a Vietnam vet. I put my neck on the line to save a lot of your people from being tortured by communists in Vietnam. Saw a lot of my buddies get blown up to pieces in the jungle. Not that I didn't do my share of killing too. The war was a terrible time. Did you know that more second-lieutenants died in Vietnam than privates? It's true. Runts didn't know better so they exercised caution, but second-lieutenants, snooty s.o.b.'s from military schools, thought they were invincible, so bam! They were the first to bite the bullet. Anyway, I'd appreciate whatever you could spare, son."

It took me a moment to realize that he was asking for money. I reached into my pockets and came up with a coin with His Excellency's picture on both sides.

"What the hell is this?" asked the man.

"I'm sorry," I said.

"Ain't you got any real money, son?"

"I'm sorry. My parents are still looking for work."

The man stared at me for a moment longer, then held up his ukulele and shook it until a Bazooka Joe popped out from inside.

He handed it to me, then trudged back toward his dumpster. Just before he crawled back inside, he turned around and said, "By the way, son. You don't want to mess with that boy. He's a wild dog masquerading as a little boy and he'll tear your head off."

CHAPTER 17
Small Pox and Ebola

The first thing next morning, I returned to the same alley. Even if the boy who had beaten me were a wild dog, I was determined to vindicate myself. After dissecting my humiliating loss overnight, I had concluded that I hadn't been aggressive enough. I had let the enemy strike the first blow and take the lead, when it was I who should have attacked first.

The boy with green and brown eyes was sitting on a milk crate, calmly reading a comic book. Around him, the other wild children were wrestling with one another playfully. They all turned to me with expressions of surprise and amusement. It was clear that they hadn't expected me to show up.

The boy handed the comic book to a lackey and began walking toward me. "You didn't chicken out. I'm impressed."

"I don't make idle threats," I said.

"Good."

I waited until he was six feet away, then lunged at him before he could ready himself. I hit him square in the stomach, but the boy seemed unfazed.

"You gotta do better than that," he said.

I swung my fists wildly and rushed at him again, hoping that luck would be on my side, but he dodged my blows expertly and kicked me repeatedly in the head.

Less than a minute later, a solid head-butt crashed into my ribs and I was once again knocked out on my back. I knew three ribs were broken before I even hit the ground. I clenched my teeth tightly and fought to keep myself from moaning in pain. I didn't want to give my enemy the pleasure of knowing that he had hurt me.

As he'd done on the previous day, my opponent peered at me from above and asked, "Enough?"

I shook my head and muttered, "This fight isn't over. I'll get you tomorrow."

He smiled sheepishly and walked away, leaving me to wallow alone. Once again, the sky above me was dark. Once again, the tall white man crawled out of the green dumpster with his ukulele and gave me a Bazooka Joe.

For the next five weeks, I returned to the alley each morning to face off against a seemingly unbeatable foe. Always, I took the first swing, and always, the boy with green and brown eyes knocked me flat on my back. Each fight ended more quickly than the preceding one. Each fight seemed to make him stronger while robbing me of my strength. Soon, I came to marvel at the fact that I had once lasted three minutes against him. Despite these discouraging developments, I cherished each and every fight. There was a perverse but visceral joy in hitting and being hit. Moreover, I knew that every blow I struck or received was preparing me for the eventual war against His Excellency that I knew I would soon wage.

After knocking me down for the 38th time, my nemesis peered at me from above and asked, "Haven't you had enough already?"

"I'm going to beat you someday. I don't know how and I don't know when, but I will. Then I'm going to fight and kill His Excellency."

He shook his head out of exasperation and scratched the back of his head. "I don't know what the hell you just said, but you're the most stubborn s.o.b. I've ever beat up."

"Go to hell," I said, getting up slowly from the ground.

He chuckled and said, "Look, man. It's silly for us to go through this day after day. No one's even watching anymore." He pointed to the other wild children. They were either writing graffiti on the walls or quietly reading comic books. No one seemed to care at all that we'd just fought.

I couldn't blame them for not paying attention to our show-downs. The spontaneity had long fizzled out of them. My opponent knew his part and I knew mine, and we raced through them as if we were participating in a carefully orchestrated ballet. I got up from the ground and patted dust off of myself.

"Let's call it quits. What d'you say?" the boy with green and brown eyes said good-naturedly. He then thrust his hand out at me. "My name's Rex."

I stared at his hand for a long while. It was small and frail just like my own, and I doubted that anyone could truly fathom just how much damage it could do. A part of me wanted to drive a screwdriver through his palm. Another part of me wanted to examine it under a microscope to learn just how it was capable of so much damage. But I did neither. Instead, I shook it and said, "I'm Boy Genius."

He repeated the name to himself and chuckled. "From your name, I guess you must be either super smart or super stupid."

"It's just a name. It doesn't mean anything."

He nodded to himself, then took out a pack of Lucky Strikes. He handed me a cigarette and lit it for me. I sucked in the smoke slowly, savoring the taste. It was my first cigarette since becoming an exile. Like everything else in North America, the cigarette was stronger and more lethal than the tobacco I'd had back in the Land of Morning Calm.

After taking a long drag, Rex said, "You ever kill anyone?"

I thought about lying, but just shook my head.

"Well, you fight pretty good regardless. Who taught you to fight like that, anyway?"

"Choco Joe," I said.

"Choco who?" He cringed his eyebrows.

"Choco Joe. He's the baddest ex-G.I. in Seoul. Everybody knows better than to mess with him."

"Well, whoever he is, he taught you pretty good. No one's ever fought me like you did. At least no boy ever did."

"I'm no boy."

"Right, right. You're no boy. You said this Choco Joe taught you to fight in Seoul. Is that where you lived before?"

"Yeah."

"You ever eat dog?"

The question caught me off guard, but I quickly answered it the way I'd been taught to do by the Central Invasion Committee in Seoul. "I've never eaten a dog in my life. Only Japanese eat dogs. I'm Korean."

He turned to the others. "Well, what do you think? Is Boy Genius tough enough to run with a gang of clever wild dogs?"

Without a word, the other children came up to me one by one and shook my hand. As if to commemorate the moment, Abraham Tomic popped out from the dumpster. From inside his ukulele he took out a dozen firecrackers and set them off. He strummed the instrument and screeched, "Kung fu comes from China! Do monks eat Aunt Ja-mima? Karate or kung fuey! Both can kill yo daddy!"

It was the first real welcome I got in Bogota.

CHAPTER 18
DMZ

Rex and his gang of wild children lived in a forgotten three-acre lot that lay adjacent to the railroad tracks. This forsaken parcel of real estate had been appropriated from Bogota's Transportation Authority and was covered with jagged rocks, broken bottles, old tires, and a thousand strains of mutant weeds that were immune to the deluge of pesticides that poured down weekly from an unmarked helicopter that belonged to Bogota's Secret Police, the biggest and most ruthless gang in town.

At first, I was reluctant to take Rex and his gang at their word that they were, indeed, clever wild dogs who had learned to masquerade as children, but the more I got to know them, the more I saw that they were actually telling the truth.

Rex slept in an abandoned yellow VW Beetle that sat on top of four cinder blocks. On the side of this makeshift shelter was spray-painted, in bright red comic-book letters, "TRAITORS MUST DIE."

The others slept mostly under trees or out in the open. They were a motley group. Some had been abandoned by their owners, cast out to the streets when a fickle child discovered an allergy. Others with iron wills had escaped their masters. A lucky few had been born wild and free and had never known the degrading tug of a leash. It didn't matter to me that they and I were members of different species. All that mattered was that unlike humans, they would be loyal to the end.

We played marathon games of kick-the-can, rob-the-blind-man, and make-precious-children-eat-sand. We ambushed unsuspecting children on their way to the orthodontist and stole their gold coins. We graffitied out stop signs and jammed subway token slots with Bazooka Joes. We tore out pages from phone books and Xeroxed twenty-dollar bills. We commandeered the el to the five-cent pool. There, we swam and peed in the same pure chlorinated water where golden-haired Normans and Rockwells had once competed for coveted spots on the U.S. Olympic team. Instead of medals, we combed the pool's depths for pennies, silver dollars, and the occasional fourteen-karat gold-plated chain. We taught impressionable children to smoke and curse and steal and masturbate and play hooky and yell at their fathers and get high at twelve and have sex at thirteen and run away from home and grow up weak and afraid and fat and medicated just like their stupid parents who hated them and each other.

We threw a thousand rocks and bottles at the silver bullet train that raced spitefully through our banlieue, ferrying passengers in crisp suits from their homes in East and West Egg to cushy jobs in Metropolis. Their crisp blue suits, their shiny leather briefcases, their hundred-dollar cuff links, their starched shirts, and the indelible sneers on their smug faces which they'd inherited from their parents, forever reminded us that we were criminals by virtue of birth and thus relegated forever to the shadow of their capital.

In the dead of night, we descended on the houses of our neighbors like angels of death. With camouflage paint on our faces and machetes in our hands, we smashed lightbulbs and threw rocks through windows, and no amount of blood on any door ever made us pass any house over.

Feeble old men, who smoked rancid cigars and sipped cheap wino wine out of crumpled paper bags, grumbled and chased us futilely with broomsticks. Defeated and broken, all they could do was give us the finger, even as arthritis ate away at their bones, and yell, through rotting gums, "Go back to China, you damn cockroaches!"

In return, we slipped firecrackers into their mailboxes and threw their cats down elevator shafts. And, in the quiet hours of the early morning, we smashed their windows and shouted, in a voice we didn't know we possessed, "Lock your doors and keep your firstborn away from the streets, cracker, 'cuz the Third World is waiting outside to ram its angry fist down your throats, torch your precious homes, destroy your manhood, and turn your perfect children against you! And when that time comes, pray to your TV for mercy for nothing will be passed over, not one damn motherfucking thing! As the old saying goes, your time has come, this is Dien Bien Phu, the Viet Cong have stormed the Embassy, your rubber plantations are no more, and revenge is sweetest when it comes from an army of roaches and clever wild dogs who have destroyed your treasures and taken your children hostage!"

CHAPTER 19

Ph.D.

My carefree days as an honorary wild dog and bad-ass mother-fucker came to a premature end, when Mother, in her own uniquely stupid way, followed the exhortations of a subway sign and registered me with the Board of Education. As a result, two members of the Bogota Secret Police burst in through our door and dragged me away to P.S. 38, the only school in Bogota.

I was angry and upset, but I couldn't fault Mother entirely. I was, after all, her only child; she was a very proud woman. Though she never came out and said it, I knew that deep down in her heart, she wanted the world to acknowledge me as a genius again.

P.S. 38 was headed by Harold N. Napalm, a former West Point cadet, who wore a black patch over his left eye. The moment he set his eye on me, he said, "This boy's been running about with wild dogs. He's got to be broken at once."

I was immediately handcuffed and gagged with duct tape and sent to a classroom headed by Ms. Sommers, an owlish white woman who never went anywhere without the trusted silver whistle that she wore around her neck. Ms. Sommers's star pupil was a ruthless four-eyed monster with an above-average I.Q. named Judy Kim, who stood three-foot-five on her tippy-toes and didn't deign to speak to those who didn't make the honor roll. She claimed to be the direct descendant of King Sejong, the ancient ruler who had invented the Hermit Kingdom's elegant writing system, a totally phonetic creature that allowed his subjects to free themselves from the yoke and oppression of Chinese pictograms.

On my first day of school, Judy stood up proudly in front of the class and read her prize-winning essay: "What I Did This Summer, by Judy Kim. I went to Korea last summer. I didn't want to go, but my parents made me. They said I had to visit my grandmother before she died. I hated it. It was hot and rainy. It smelled of cockroaches, with rats all over. There were no sewers and the people didn't have anything—no arms, no legs, no eyes. I can't believe my parents actually come from there. I'm looking forward to studying hard this year. The end."

Through the entire essay, she stared right at me and sent me telepathic messages that said she couldn't stand the sight of my bowed legs and my yellow-earth Pearl-Buck teeth, both gifts which I'd inherited from two hundred generations of peasants.

Meanwhile, Napalm's trusted team of cronies tried their best to break me into submission with sophisticated techniques culled from heavy textbooks and psychology journals issued weekly by the Board of Education. But theory didn't coincide with reality. No occupying force could have been more ill-prepared to face my wrath. I knew firsthand from two-dozen wars fought by my brethren against imperialist Western regimes that victory was gained not by military might or strategic advantage but by the power of the will. In contrast, P.S. 38's teachers had grown up weak and soft, nestled in the walls of cozy Levittown; their minds and souls had long ago been lost to the cushioned credit-card comfort of the television age.

I parried their every blow and answered their feeble fire with a barrage of ICBMs fired from the great battle-ready deck of my personal battleship, the S.S. Motherfucker.

On a chilly autumn morning, just minutes after the President, a former actor who'd starred in a dozen B-movies, ordered the invasion of an insignificant Central American country to commemorate Columbus Day, Ms. Sommers exhorted the class to recite poems of tribute to the Italian navigator.

Led by Judy Kim, the class began, in their mindless sing-song voices, *"In 1492, Columbus sailed the Ocean Blue . . ."*

I'm not sure if it was the shrill sound of Judy's voice or the sight of her and Ms. Sommers standing there, so smug and prim, that triggered it, but the rage that had built up inside of me since my fall from grace detonated into a mushroom cloud like none that Bogota had ever seen.

I wiggled my hands free from the handcuffs that held me to the steaming radiator in the back of the room, ripped off the duct tape that gagged my mouth, and shouted in crystal-clear digital Dolby Stereo Surroundsound, "In 1492, Columbus sailed the Ocean Blue, because he was a tool of the European colonialist regime that led the way for the rape of the New World and the genocide of the indigenous people. As for the Niña, the Pinta, and the Santa Maria, they were ships of destruction like the U.S.S. Intrepid and the U.S.S. Arizona, ready to loot and pillage and kill and enslave the New World. As for Columbus's title as an explorer, he never even reached India, which was his destination. He never even came close. He was off by 10,000 miles."

The entire class stared at me in disbelief. Ms. Sommers shook violently and shouted, "I didn't call on you, Boy Genius!"

"I never said you did. I called on myself for I am that I am. As for the mighty British and the Anglo-Saxon empire, in which the sun allegedly never set, they were the biggest drug dealers of their day, worse than a thousand Colombian cartels. The famous British East India Company, on which your textbooks heap endless praise, grew opium in India and pimped it on the Chinese. They were drug dealers of the worst kind . . ."

"That's enough, Boy Genius. I will not let you talk disparagingly about the British East India Company. You're going to pay for this, you little brat." Ms. Sommers then brought her silver whistle to her mouth.

The ensuing high-pitched shriek pierced the air, and immediately Mr. Baker, the gym teacher, and Mr. Sanchez, the custodian, raced inside. They exchanged glances with Ms. Sommers, then lunged at me. For the next two minutes, I grappled with these two burly middle-aged ex–high school wrestlers with all the strength of my young body. Through it all, Judy Kim shouted, again and again, "Kick the punk's ass!"

Despite Judy's eager exhortations, my opponents didn't fare well. They underestimated my strength, and my wild dog training had made me tougher than any boy should be. Indeed, were it not for the illegal chokeholds that they had learned from a secret pamphlet distributed by the Board of Education, I might very well have outwrestled them.

Once I was pinned to the ground, Mr. Baker and Mr. Sanchez lifted me by my feet and carried me down to the basement.

There, Principal Napalm greeted me in front of an ancient black coal furnace that made a soft hissing sound as it cast an eerie orange glow in the room. Next to him was a rust-covered film projector that looked like it had been assembled personally by the Wizard of Menlo Park at the beginning of the century. Without a word, Principal Napalm turned it on. A beam of white light shone on the wall, the reels began to spin around noisily, and a picture of an Asian boy in tattered rags appeared on the opposite wall. The boy looked to be about six years old and was doing cartwheels around a dirt yard. He looked very familiar, and I couldn't help wondering if I had met him back in Star Village.

"Isn't it something, Boy Genius? I say, isn't it something?" Napalm said above the hum of the projector. "Look at the rags on him. It's like looking head-on at the face of the Depression. You should consider yourself fortunate, Boy Genius. Extremely fortunate."

I couldn't take my eyes off the boy on the wall. There had been a hundred boys just like him in the shantytown where Mother had cried for me. The boy stopped doing cartwheels and grinned stupidly at the camera. Then, from the edge of the frame, a little girl with one leg hopped up to him and handed him a clear plastic bag filled with green flies.

"My goodness, would you look at that that? Now, how do you suppose she lost that leg?" asked Napalm.

I didn't say anything.

"I'll tell you how. She probably got it blown up playing in some field when a forgotten landmine went off. Things like that happen after a war, you know. Wars end, but the casualties go on and on. Why, I wouldn't be surprised if a mine went off today in your country and blew some poor kid's arms off."

Napalm turned off the projector and walked slowly up to me. He drew a finger slowly across my cheek and said, "That boy could easily have been you. Did you ever think about that?"

"Go to hell!" I shouted, struggling in vain to free myself from Mr. Baker and Mr. Sanchez's grip.

Napalm shook his head, calmly reached inside his suit, and took out a cigar. After lighting it, he said, "I knew you were going to cause headaches the moment I saw you. Just because you were a genius in your country doesn't mean you're one here."

"Go to hell! You're nothing more than a pathetic white man who's failed to conquer the world. Your wife hates you and your mother never loved you and your work never meant a damn thing. Your gods are dead and your life has no meaning. When your children start making more money than you they will call you a loser and treat you like an invalid. How do you live with yourself?"

Napalm blew a cloud of cigar smoke right in my face. Instantly, the smell of dead Cubans filled the room. "You really should show more respect to me. After all, I fought a war for you."

"Murderer!" I cried out. "You're a murderer! You gunned down innocent villagers at No Gun Ri! You slaughtered women and children at No Gun Ri! You killed my parents at No Gun Ri!"

He smiled and removed his eye patch, then took out his glass eye, blew on it softly, and began wiping it with a handkerchief. "I know for a fact that your parents are alive and well, Boy Genius. I spoke with them this morning. They're very nice people, hardworking and well-mannered. I understand your mother now runs a ramen stall at the East Gate Market and your father is a rickshaw driver at West Gate."

It was true. Every morning, before they scurried away to earn a few dollars, they'd tell me, "Try not to get in trouble today."

Every night, they'd return, more tired and old than the night before, and say, "Just a few more dollars and we'll be able to live in a house next to white people."

Napalm shook his head and sighed. "It's difficult to understand how a malcontent like you could come from such good stock. Anyway, they gave me their blessing to make sure you learn your lesson once and for all. So I'm willing to do whatever it takes to teach you a little discipline and respect."

"Murderer! You killed innocent babies during the war! You slept with prostitutes and beat up old men! You supported regimes that killed thousands of innocent people. Had you not supplied His Excellency with guns and food, had Theodore Roosevelt never sold out the Hermit Kingdom to the Japanese in exchange for U.S. control of the Philippines, had JFK never felt compelled to help the French because they spoke with a fancy accent, His Excellency might have lived out his life as a schoolteacher instructing snot-nosed children how to read, instead of concocting five-year plans and mobilizing the masses; our peninsula might never have needed geniuses, and I might never have been forced to flee my homeland like some defective transistor radio with 'Made in Korea' stamped on its back! You may not see it, but there's definitely blood on your hands!"

He popped his glass eye back into its socket and put the patch back on. "Blood on my hands, you say? Do you know that I filmed this footage in person? We were at a village just south of Seoul in the winter of '50. Those were grand times. I was nineteen and in the prime of my youth. Thought I could do anything. There were real men back then, not just suits out for money. We fought and risked our lives for ideas. That's how life is, son. Great men concern themselves with ideas. Ordinary men busy themselves with events. And inferior men occupy themselves with things. General Douglas MacArthur taught me that. You know who he is, don't you? There's a statue of him in Inchon and at the U.S. Military Academy in West Point. Your countrymen aren't the only ones who think of him as a hero, you know. Had he had his way, the Korean conflict would have ended with China becoming our fifty-first state and there would have never been a Vietnam War. What an adventure that was. Sure there were some bad apples among us. But there always are. Did some innocent peasants die needlessly? Of course. We were just kids, after all, eighteen- and nineteen-year-olds. For most of us, it was the first time we'd ever been outside the States. For a lot of the boys in my platoon, Seoul was the first real city they'd set eyes on. We might have gotten carried away at times. Shots were fired at random groups of people, regardless of whether they were from the South or from the North. But do I regret it? Hell no! It was the turning point of my life. Had I not gone to fight, I might very well have enjoyed a long career as a gas station attendant or a no-good hobo. And that's no exaggeration. Never let anyone tell you war is bad, son. War isn't bad. If you die and lose, it's one thing, but if you win and live to talk about it, war's just about the best thing that can ever happen to you. The best damn thing. Every strong nation needs a war now and then to test its mettle. Otherwise, you become slow and weak."

"Like you. Slow and weak."

He stared at me with venom for a long while, then said, "Yes, that's right. Like me. Slow and weak. But I'm still strong enough to deal with a little punk who doesn't know what's best for him."

He walked behind me. Then, he leaned down close to my ear and said, "We can't have you yelling whatever comes to your mind in class, Boy Genius. That's just not how things are done here. It's not fair to your teacher, and it's not fair to the other children. Do you understand me?"

"I understand that you're a homosexual. That's why you enjoyed the army so much."

He groaned and pressed the tip of his cigar into the middle of my back. The dime-sized tip felt cold as if I were being stabbed with an icicle.

"I didn't want it to get like this, Boy Genius. I really didn't, but you give me no choice. Words are fine and dandy, but nothing gets one's point across as well as physical pain. That's a lesson I learned while pumping bullets into the Chinese near the Yalu. It's also been documented in study after study by prominent psychologists throughout the world."

The smell of roasting cuttlefish wafted through the room and made me nauseous. Fighting this sensation, I managed to feign a hearty laugh and said, "Burn me all you want, you'll never beat me. I'll win in the end, just like the Chinese you couldn't drive out of Korea and the North Vietnamese you couldn't drive out of Ho Chi Minh City."

"Saigon! The city is called Saigon!"

"Ho Chi Minh City," I repeated, stressing every syllable.

Napalm groaned, then pressed the cigar even harder into my back. "The damn city's called Saigon."

CHAPTER 20
Bogota Hilton

My private meetings with Napalm continued daily for many months. During this time, Napalm pressed hot metal rods against my back and etched excerpts from classic works cited by experts to have contributed to the development of democracy in the Western world. The resulting pain was unbearable, but Napalm's plan to turn me into a walking monument was doomed for failure.

Fueled by the tide of dark revolution that had begun with Genghis Khan's conquest of Europe right through Haiti's victory over Napoleon and culminating in Indochina's victory over *les Oncles Charles et Sam,* my back grew thick and hard like a slab of impenetrable Third World granite, and no more words could be etched.

Unwilling to admit defeat, Napalm dragged me to the school's subbasement and shoved me into a dark utility closet, just wide enough for me to sit down with my knees tucked under my chin. Every 38 minutes, a buzzer sounded, a bolt of electricity coursed through my body, and a robust Midwestern voice sang, *"Might makes right and right makes might. Bow before your master."*

Despite the fact that I was being held against my will, the darkness was, at first, comforting. It enveloped me and allowed me the leisure that I so desperately needed to collect my thoughts. Like old prisoners who've spent nearly all their lives in cages, I came to feel almost safe in captivity. But this sense of ease and comfort was deceptive and quickly turned into a slow but steady suffocation. I longed to see something, anything, and I yearned to hear the sound of something that wasn't the recording or my own voice.

Just when I thought I would surely wither away to nothing, Napalm dragged me up a secret set of stairs to the roof.

The sun seemed to glower at me from above and it took my eyes a long time to get readjusted to its harsh rays. The surrounding rooftops were filled with twisted antennas and makeshift clotheslines on which a flock of soiled laundry fluttered in the wind. Thick black smoke billowed from incinerator chimneys as if in slow motion, and ancient wooden water towers the size of elephants sat ominously on top of rusty metal scaffolding.

Napalm pointed west to the magnificent skyscrapers that loomed against the sky. It was difficult to believe that these mammoth monuments that seemed to stretch endlessly into the heavens had been made without slaves. They spoke to me of the power that Bogota's rulers had. A country that had built the A-bomb was capable of anything.

With a smug expression, Napalm said, "Give up your silly resistance, Boy Genius, and all the world can be yours. A fighting spirit is good, often commendable. But one must also be able to recognize when it's time to give up and capitulate. Even the Emperor of Japan who lived as a god amongst his people knew when his time was up. There's no dishonor in surrender, only in foolish stubbornness. Bow down before me and renounce this futile cause of yours that's gone the way of the dodo bird, the oil lamp, and the horse-drawn carriage, and one day you will be rewarded with an important position in society. You'll become somebody."

I pretended to be impressed and started to bow to him. But before my torso was parallel to the floor, I turned and quickly ran to the opposite edge of the roof. Then, before a stunned Napalm could stop me, I unzipped my pants and let loose a stream of bright yellow Third World urine that traveled down the side of the building in a perfect parabola before landing flush on Judy Kim's head. She touched her hair and looked up quizzically. I smiled and waved my uncircumcised pepper at her, and she let forth a scream that made the entire schoolyard stop and stare.

Then, Tanh Uhung, a Vietnamese refugee who had endured pirates and starvation to come to America, and who was making slow but steady progress in P.S. 38's marvelous ESL program, pointed to the sky and shouted, "Lookie, everyone! A rainbow! Hello, Roy G. Biv!"

There, indeed, was a glorious rainbow in the sky, but I couldn't admire its beauty or ruminate on the whereabouts of the pot of gold at its end for long. Napalm yanked me back from the roof's edge and glared at me through his one eye. "Have it your way, Boy Genius. We'll see who comes out on top in the end. I was merely trying to save you from unnecessary suffering and cruel and unusual punishment, but you've forced my hand. The ball was in your court. Now you've sealed your fate, and I'm afraid you're going to regret this little stunt of yours."

I smiled and said, "Fuck thou, motherfucker! Fuck thou!"

Shaking his head, Napalm dragged me back to the subbasement and returned me to darkness.

CHAPTER 21
Taco Choco

Darkness became my only reality, and even the faces of Mother and Father faded from my memory. Then, just when I began to fear that I would die a forgotten P.O.W. in an underground room just eight miles away from the Statue of Liberty, to which a legion of *les enfants stupides* had contributed, a gravelly but familiar voice called out to me.

"How you doing, kid? I see they've got you in a bind here."

"Who said that?" I shouted into the darkness.

"It's me, kid."

I stabbed at the darkness and felt a shoulder. It was thin and bony.

"Easy there, kid. Don't squeeze so hard. I'm not going anywhere." The figure lit a cigarette. A pair of worn boxing gloves was draped around his neck.

"Choco Joe!" I shouted.

He set the box of matches next to him and said, "Would you believe this here is my billionth cigarette? I've been trying to quit for a long time now, but I guess it's like Mark Twain once said, 'Quitting smoking is the easiest thing in the world. I've done it hundreds of times.'" He sucked on the cigarette and handed me the match.

"Is it really you, Choco Joe?" I held the flame close to his face. His hair had turned gray around the temples, but his face was the same, as shiny as the outside of an eggplant with no trace of a wrinkle, not even around the corners of his eyes.

"Sure it's me. Who else would be wearing this shit?" He picked up the box of matches and lit another one. He then motioned for me to blow out my match.

I did so, then said, "I can't believe it's you, Choco Joe. I can't believe it's really you."

"Believe it, kid." The flame ate its way up the thin match toward Choco Joe's bony fingers. With the other hand, he handed me his cigarette.

I sucked on it with all the force of my lungs. It was the tastiest cigarette I'd ever had in my life.

"I had a hard time finding you," Choco Joe continued. "Searched all over the world for you, kid. All seven continents, and ninety-six countries. You wouldn't believe the things that are going on in the world at this very moment, kid. People are slaughtering one another and trying to turn the weak into slaves. And it's not just here. It's everywhere. Everywhere. And what for? For nickels and potatoes. We're the only life form on the planet that kills and tortures because we don't like how someone looks. That's why my ancestors were slaves and your country was split up between the U.S. and the Soviet Union. Somewhere back in history, some sorry bastard decided he just didn't like how someone looked. That's the only reason they dropped the big one on Hiroshima and not on Berlin."

"Hiroshima?"

"Yeah, kid, Hiroshima. That's where they dropped the big one in W-W-II. From a plane called the Enola Gay. It's the only time that the power of the atom's ever been harnessed against a people. And it happened 'cuz some guy who makes decisions decided he didn't like how the Jap looked. But I'll tell you it won't be like that in the future. No way. Science will make sure of it. Even as we speak, the greatest minds of the world are working around the clock in high-tech secret laboratories in Moscow, Pyoungyang, Hiroshima, and Los Alamos to develop a way to turn white men black and black men white and vice versa. Why? Not because of some desire to allow man to transcend the particular markings of race or to bring about peace on earth, but to enhance their respective nations' elaborate intelligence-gathering efforts. But you can rest assured that enterprising minds will find innovative applications for these break-throughs. Someday, not too long from now, you'll be able to walk into a storefront clinic at your local mall and decide what color skin you want. When that happens, it won't matter a mound of beans what your skin color is or what race you happened to be born with. People will change their skin color and their facial features as often and with as much frivolity as they would the color of their hair."

"Do you really think that'll happen, Choco Joe?"

"I know it'll happen. It has to. If it doesn't, we'll have World War III, with races fighting one another in every city and state. Anyway, no more talk about race wars. I don't want to get you down. Let me take a good look at you, kid."

"I've grown six inches since I last saw you, Choco Joe. I'm almost as tall as you are."

"You've shot up quite a bit. But you're all skin and bones. You're almost as thin as Choco Joe."

"I'm trapped here all day."

"It ain't right, kid. Whatever you might have done, you're still just a kid. The bastards who locked you up down here are dogs, I tell you. These bastards are dogs."

I shook my head forcefully. "Don't say that, Choco Joe. I know dogs, and dogs aren't like this. They aren't like this at all."

Choco Joe stared at me with a sad expression. I blew a puff of smoke the way Choco Joe had taught me to so many years back. It floated between us and formed the letters KBS.

Choco Joe smiled. "Not bad, kid. Not bad. It looks like you still got the stuff."

He threw the match away and lit another. He kept lighting new matches when the last one was nearly out. For a long while, both of us watched the flame and said nothing. Then, I said, "Why did they sell me out, Choco Joe? Why did they take me off the air?"

Choco Joe cringed. "I was afraid you'd ask me that. It's a long story, kid, and we don't have time to get into it right now. But you'll get all the details soon. You can trust me on that."

"I only did what I was supposed to do. I only did what they asked me. That's what I was supposed to do, wasn't I?"

"Sure, kid. You did good. You did real good."

"Then why did His Excellency cast me aside like a pair of old socks?"

Shaking his head, he said, "Here's the deal, kid. There were forces at work bigger than you or me. You were a shrimp caught between two whales who were out for blood. But forget all that. It does you no good to dwell on that stuff now."

"I can't help but dwell on it. It changed my life overnight."

He reached into his boxing glove and took out a Hershey's bar. He broke it in half and said, "Here, kid. Have some of this."

I took the half from him and said, "Thanks, Choco Joe. I'm glad you're here."

"So am I, kid." He ripped the wrapping off his half and popped the chocolate in his mouth.

"Commie bastards must be killed without mercy."

Choco Joe stared at me intently. "What'd you say, kid?"

"Long live His Excellency the Most Honorable President Park. The U.S.A. is our number-one friend and ally in everything. Remember, Choco Joe? Remember?"

"Sure, I remember, kid."

"I was so stupid. You were right all along, Choco Joe. His Excellency was a bad man. You were right all along."

"Forget it, kid. It doesn't matter who was right and who was wrong. All that's in the past. What you gotta focus on now is your future."

"I want to help communists, Choco Joe. I want to help communists overthrow His Excellency's regime."

"Forget it, kid. There are no communists left. Not in Korea and not in the U.S.A. Dialectical materialism's just an empty word. It's all over. Winners win and losers lose. That's how it's always been, and that's how it'll always be. There's no use in trying to change what can't be changed."

"You sent me oranges, Choco Joe. You were the only one who

came to me after I was thrown out of KBS. You were the only one."

He touched my arm and shook me gently. "Snap out of it, kid."

"Remember the time you came over to my house for Chinese New Year? All the neighborhood kids just went crazy. They put us on their shoulders and carried us down the street. We threw coins off of my roof and watched the street urchins nearly kill each other for them. Remember?"

He crossed his arms over his chest, hunching his shoulders. "Listen, Boy Genius. You gotta snap out of this. I like to reminisce as much as the next man, but all these memories just ain't doing you no good. You gotta look to your future, not the past."

"I can't forget. I tried, but I just can't."

"Then try harder. Otherwise, you'll end up like Choco Joe, a bitter old soldier with no family, no children, no home, with nothing to show for himself except his dog tags and his boxing gloves."

"I can't control what I remember and what I forget, Choco Joe."

Choco Joe stared at me. Even in the dim light, I could see the red veins that covered his eyeballs.

"Fine, kid. Have it your way. You've buttered your bread, now you better lie in it. But you listen to me, and listen good. What happened to you wasn't right. But it wasn't your fault. You were at an impressionable age, and His Excellency was pretty damn persuasive. But that era's over and done with, gone forever."

"What d'you mean, gone forever?"

"I don't know how to tell you this, kid, so I'll just come out and say it. His Excellency is *kaputt.*"

"What?"

"His Excellency is *kaputt. Finito. Nicht mere. Sayonara. Adiós muchachos.* Gone."

"I don't understand."

"He was gunned down by the head of the KCIA at a private dinner attended by his closest inner circle. He was pumped full of bullets and died whimpering, like a mangy dog."

"But that can't be."

"That's the way it went down, kid."

"He's not supposed to die like that. Not like that."

"I understand, kid. You wanted to kill him yourself, right?"

"He abandoned me, Choco Joe. He was supposed to be my friend. He was supposed to be my father."

"I know, kid, I know."

"I hate Him. I hate Him so much."

Choco Joe sighed. "So you hated him. So did a lot of people. You gotta put aside whatever private war you had against him and start thinking about yourself. 'Cuz when it comes right down to it, there ain't no such thing as country, family, or friend. It's just you versus the world. And no matter how bad you feel about the way things are going, you gotta sit up and remember that time will cure pretty much everything and Choco Joe wants you to live to see another day. You hear me?"

I nodded.

"Then say it with me, Boy Genius," he paused. "Choco Joe wants me to live."

"Choco Joe wants me to live," I said, turning each word over in my head.

"Good. Now say it again. Choco Joe . . . "

"Choco Joe wants me to live. Choco Joe wants me to live. Choco Joe . . . Choco Joe?"

The room was dark again, and all was quiet. I stabbed the darkness again with my hands, but the only bony shoulder in the room was mine. Choco Joe was gone and I was alone again.

CHAPTER 22

Population vs. Invention

The deprivation of solitary confinement and the news of His Excellency's sudden death sapped me of my strength and resolve. The only thing that had sustained me in my exiled life until then had been the feint hope of someday carrying out the sentence I'd passed against His Excellency. Now that this possibility was no more, I had nothing to live for. I began preparing for death. But this was not to be.

Fearing that I would die while in captivity and become a martyr for the many oppressed groups who formed secret alliances throughout Bogota, Napalm released me just before the brink of death and had me rejoin the student population. I complied without a fight.

Little had changed in Ms. Sommers's class. Judy Kim's hand was still raised. The walls were still covered with glossy pictures of all the U.S. presidents. A map that pulled down from the top ledge of the blackboard showed the countries that the U.S. had helped with generous financial and military aid throughout history. And students were gathered in clusters engrossed in Monopoly, Beat the Bank, and other clever games designed to lull them into submission and train them for future employment.

So it's come to this, I said to myself, then took a seat in the back next to Tanh Uhung, the mild-mannered boatchild from Vietnam. He smiled and handed me a Bazooka Joe. I thanked him and began the day's do-now, copying the times table.

Slowly, the memory of my wild past faded away from the annals of P.S. 38's history. Napalm, Ms. Sommers, and my classmates, with the exception of Judy Kim, came to see me as just another well-mannered boy from the Orient. Much of the credit for this smooth transition was owed to Tanh. Whenever it appeared that I might relapse into the old me and act out like a wild dog, he pulled me aside and said, "Lookie, Boy Genius. As bad as things may are, no forget we much better off than ghetto black. Someday, you and I gonna be bigshot and live in big mansion. Ghetto black have nothing and get shot by police. So be patient and go with flow, man. You acting bad-ass gonna make it hard for rest of us."

Despite the fact that Tanh had been born in the jungles of an insignificant Third World country ravaged by centuries of European colonialism, I took his advice to heart. After all, he and I weren't that different. We were both eyewitnesses to the unspeakable devastation that communism could wreak on a country, and we would always be mistaken for loyal subjects of the Middle Kingdom by the other residents of Bogota: hairy Sicilians, angry blacks, and dirty Puerto Ricans. Most importantly, had Tanh been born in Korea with a much higher I.Q., he and I might have been cousins.

Following Tanh's example, I always smiled and said thank you to P.S. 38's staff of white teachers. I did my homework on time and always answered the extra-credit question. I no longer shouted out in class, and I no longer called Napalm a murderer. I was the prodigal gook who had returned to the fold. I was the P.O.W. who had been compelled by reason and the power of truth, justice, and baseball to lay down his arms and dedicate his life to maintaining peace and order.

After a class trip to the Museum of Natural History, where bones of ancient animals were displayed in large glass boxes, a disheveled black man walked up to me while our class was eating lunch in a public park. Parts of six combs were sticking out of his prominent afro, and he was brandishing a squeegee as if it were a sword. Grinning widely through sparkling white teeth, this descendant of African slaves and resident of the city's secret underground tunnels cackled loudly, then pointed to the sky.

Directly above us, a Goodyear blimp was flying slowly across and momentarily eclipsed the sun, sending us into darkness.

When the sun returned, the black man held up his squeegee as if it were an Uzi, and shouted, "Rat-ta-ta-ta-tat, my friend! A plane from your country was just shot down by the Ruskies this morning. Sayonara to 147 passengers. The Ruskies claim it was a spy plane out to steal military secrets. The White House says Nikolai and Ivan did it in cold blood, which makes them worse than wild dogs. Either way, all signs lead to the same conclusion. We're on the brink of double-u, double-u three. Rat-ta-ta-ta-tat, my friend!"

Alarmed by the sudden commotion, Ms. Sommers rushed over frantically from the other side of the park and glared at the homeless man. "What're you doing?" she shouted at him. "Do you want me to call the police?"

The tall African lowered his squeegee, mumbled incoherently, then stumbled away. Ms. Sommers stared after him, then turned to me. "Are you okay, Boy Genius?"

"I'm fine, Ms. Sommers."

"Did that man say anything to you?"

"He said a plane was shot down this morning. He said he was glad my relatives were dead."

"You didn't really lose anyone on that plane, did you?"

I looked down at the ground and mumbled, "Just a few cousins."

She sighed. "I'm so sorry, Boy Genius."

"It's okay. It wasn't your fault. It was the Russians. They shot the plane down in cold blood. Everywhere in this world, communists are killing people who look like me."

She bent down and touched my cheeks softly. "I wish I could tell you that the world was a perfect place, Boy Genius. But it's not. There will always be communists. And there will always be tragedies and crazy black people to remind you of inequalities and injustice. People you love will pass on and leave you behind. And there will always be those narrow-minded few who'll judge you by your appearance and not by the content of your character. But be patient and strong. Someday, science will find a way to correct your appearance. Then, you'll never have to suffer for being born where you were. Until then, your secret's safe with me. And remember, I'll always be your friend."

I nodded and said, "You're so kind, Ms. Sommers. Not at all like the other white people."

She stared at me for a long while, then pulled me tightly to her. I rested my cheeks on her soft and pillowy breasts and breathed in her fragrance. She smelled buttery, like a plate of mashed potatoes.

CHAPTER 23
The Bogota Accords

Three days after the disappearance of the Korean Airliner in the Sea of Japan, a special assembly was held at P.S. 38's cafetorium. After a moment of silence to pay respects to the dead, I got up on stage before the entire school, thrust my hand on a heavy Christian Bible, and declared, "I promise my allegiance to the powers that govern this society and swear I will never question its authority or challenge its institutions of power. I realize the errors of my past and promise never to repeat them. I have been rehabilitated and am a proud supporter of P.S. 38, the President, Congress, and the Constitution."

Amidst thunderous applause, the likes of which hadn't been heard in the halls of P.S. 38 since V-Day, I signed my name on the Bogota Accords, a document that had been drafted by Napalm, Ms. Sommers, and a committee of specialists hired by the Board of Education.

As I stood there on stage and embraced the applause, Napalm leaned down and whispered softly in my ear, "I know this must have been hard for you, Boy Genius. But one day, you're going to thank your lucky stars that you signed this. Today is the first day of the rest of your life."

The news of my surrender swept quickly through Bogota. As I walked home after school, a bevy of curious merchants, mostly dirty ethnics with greasy hair and heavy accents, stepped outside their grimy shops and clapped. Old women and new mothers pushed their strollers up to me, genuflected like ancient pilgrims, and kissed me as if I were a soldier returning triumphantly from battle. One mother, a tiny Mexican woman, struggling with a bulky stroller that held identical twins of indeterminate age, gushed, "You did the right thing, Boy Genius. The fighting was straining the barrio. Peace is always muy better than war."

These heartfelt reassurances helped somewhat to put my mind at ease, but I knew that there would be others who viewed my actions as capitulation and cowardice. Not actively fighting the enemy was one thing. Signing a formal declaration like the Bogota Accords was something else.

As I approached the entrance to the King George Luxury Apartments, Abraham Tomic popped out from behind a tree and rushed over to me. As always, he reeked of cheap booze and had his ukulele tucked under one arm.

"What's going on, Abraham?" I said.

He strummed his ukulele and sang, *"Boy Genius, you're fi-nal-ly here. Soon everything will be cle-ar. I've been wai-ting for you all day. Let's go upstairs without de-lay."*

The dark lobby reeked of fried plantains. Two teenage Mexican girls were selling this cherished South American delicacy out of a cleverly redesigned shopping cart that had been appropriated in the dead of night from the local A&P. Abraham winked at them lewdly and made obscene gestures with his pelvis. The girls giggled, then gave him the finger.

The elevator creaked loudly as it ferried Abraham and me up six flights, and the ancient fluorescent bulb overhead flickered wildly as if it were sending secret signals to extraterrestrial life forms.

"I think the girls downstairs like you, Boy Genius," said Abraham.

"Shut up," I said. Then, before Abraham could say any more, I took out a black magic marker from my back pocket and wrote *"Kill Mordechai"* on the elevator wall. It was the 38th time that I had written that particular slogan in the building.

When I opened my door and stepped inside my apartment, a thick cloud of black smoke hugged me. The entire living room was covered in ash and soot, and the walls were charred.

Abraham shook his head and said, "I spotted the fire from downstairs, but I didn't call the cops. I figured you'd want it that way."

I nodded and continued into my room.

Where my bed had been, there was now just a large pool of black liquid. Directly above it, there were two pair of feet hanging in midair. These belonged to the lifeless bodies of my parents, who were tied to the ceiling fan. Father's feet were of average size, but Mother's were extraordinarily big, as if they belonged to a Chinese national. For a moment, I stood there and wondered why I had never noticed Mother's large feet before.

Abraham lowered his head. "I'm sorry, Boy Genius. I'm very, very sorry."

I nodded and stared at Mother and Father. Their faces had been slashed beyond recognition, their insides were strewn all over the walls, and their thigh bones had been gnawed right through the marrow. On the wall behind their limp bodies, a message was written in blood, in letters that looked clearly like those found in cheap comic books: *"Traitors must die."*

I took a deep breath. "May I be alone please, Abraham?"

"Take your time, son. I'll wait outside." He turned quietly and walked out the door.

I lowered the cold limp bodies of my parents to the floor and laid them side by side. As I did so, the closet door slid open and out stepped Aunt Number Six. She had aged much since our last meeting at Kimpo Airport. Her hair was gray around the temples and there were a dozen wrinkles around the corners of her eyes. Both changes gave her face a determination that she hadn't had earlier.

She came right up to me and spat a glob of green phlegm on my face.

I didn't bother to wipe away the slime. It rolled down my left cheek, yo-yoed for a while off my chin, then fell to the floor.

"You killed them. I warned you not to, Boy Genius. But you killed them anyway."

There was nothing I could say in my defense. I'd known from

the very moment of my conception, when my father's sperm had made contact with my mother's egg in her oviduct, that my parents were too weak to survive another war. Yet, I had insisted on indulging myself in a surreptitious guerilla war against Napalm and P.S. 38. My selfishness and arrogance had sent Mother and Father to My Lai. I, a former national treasure, who had digested the wisdom of the great Kon-Fu-Tze at age three, had proven myself to be a worthless son.

I couldn't bear my aunt's accusing stare for much longer, so I ran outside. To her credit, she didn't try to stop or follow me. I ran down the stairs and continued through the lobby past Abraham and the two plantain sellers.

The same broken bottles and discarded tires were strewn all over the forgotten three-acre lot next to the railroad tracks. The same abandoned VW Beetle sat on top of cinder blocks. But there was no trace of Rex or the wild dogs. They had abandoned their camp, and I couldn't pick up their scent, no matter how desperately I searched the air.

I sat listlessly on the railroad tracks and threw pebbles at nearby shrubs until the cold metal under my behind began vibrating. From the distance, a train was racing toward me, and its whistle sounded.

For a moment, I considered lying down and letting the train run over me, but I couldn't get myself to end things that way. As saddened as I was by Mother and Father's passing, deep down, I knew that my genius was not meant to go out like that. I moved away from the tracks and watched the train race past.

A suit with a perfect haircut smiled out of the moving window and gave me the thumbs-up sign. I picked up a Coca-Cola bottle and threw it at him. It bounced off the side of the train and landed in a clump of weeds. The suit stared after me with a confused expression on his face. He had no doubt heard about the Bogota Accords and no longer considered me a threat.

After the train disappeared, a squirrel that had been born

black through industrial melanism darted around my feet and shouted, "You're not to blame, Boy Genius. You didn't know this was going to happen! It's not your fault!"

The rodent's words did little to console me. It was plain that Rex and his band of murderous wild dogs had celebrated the Bogota Accords by turning my home into a field of blood, and by butchering the only two people who had ever truly loved me.

CHAPTER 24
Chinaman's Chance

Abraham helped me bury my parents in a shady plot of earth near the VW Beetle. I marked their graves with a crude cross fashioned out of broomsticks. I knew that Mother, who had given up her clan's primitive brand of shamanism for Christianity as a child when three Iowan missionaries came knocking with chocolates and other sweets, would have appreciated the gesture.

Then, as the custom of Father's clan demanded, I placed two bags of oranges and a bottle of beer before the grave and kowtowed nine times, the way Father had done for his father on the ninth month of the lunar calendar. It was a primitive Third World ritual, but it was the only heirloom Father had managed to pass down to me.

When I was done, Abraham set off firecrackers, strummed his ukulele, and sang, *"This world sucks. The good die. The bad die. Everybody dies. All together now. This world sucks. The young die. The old die. Everybody dies."*

Afterwards, Abraham managed a weak smile and said, "I'm sorry about all this, Boy Genius. I don't know what to tell you except, I guess, you're an orphan now."

I nodded listlessly. There was no way Abraham could understand that my genius had made me an orphan since the day I was born. No matter how hard I or anyone else tried, my life had been and would continue to be different from that of other children. Poor Abraham would never appreciate that. He was happy with his booze, his firecrackers, his nonsense songs, and his fantasies about Cuba and the revolution, and I was in no position to take that kind of happiness away from him.

He scratched the back of his head and said, "Come on, Boy Genius, keep your chin up. It's not the end of the world." He set off a dozen more firecrackers, then thrust his fist high above his head and shouted, *"Viva Fidel! Viva la revolucion!"*

I held up my fist in solidarity and repeated his mantra, but the words fell lifelessly out of my mouth. I didn't believe in Fidel or the revolution. All I wanted was to have my parents back.

"You're gonna go after them, aren't you?" asked Abraham.

I kicked a rock at my feet. "They couldn't have gotten far. I'll find them and kill them."

"Revenge only begets more violence, Boy Genius. It's what the experts call the circle of violence."

"I don't care about the experts."

"Fine, Boy Genius. But tell me just one thing: How do you even know it was them who did it?"

"Come on, Abraham. You have to be stupid not to put two and two together. It's obvious, isn't it? To them, I'm a traitor. I sold them out by signing the Bogota Accords."

"No one said you were a traitor."

"No one has to."

He shook his head. "Look, Boy Genius. What happened to you happened because you grew old and the school system got their hands on you. It happens to even the best people. Not everyone can be a bad-ass forever. Not even you."

"I could have put up a better fight. I gave up too soon."

"Wins and losses. That's for future historians to decide. After what you went through, even Rex might have done the same thing."

"Rex would never have done what I did."

"Why the hell not?"

"Because."

"Because what?"

"Because Rex and I are different."

"That's true, Boy Genius. You are different. Rex didn't have a family. He wasn't even human."

"That made him tough."

"That might be. But you and him were never meant to be friends for long. He would have turned on you sooner or later. Wild dogs and humans can stay allies for only so long. After that, it's dog against man."

"I'm going after him."

"What good will that do? You might spend your entire life looking for Rex and never find him."

"I'll never find him if I don't try."

"Fine. Let's say you find him. Then what?"

"I'll kill him."

"Come on, Boy Genius. You know very well that you're no match for Rex. And don't even try to tell me otherwise. You've got a lot of guts, son, I'll hand you that, but Rex is the toughest wild dog in Bogota history. And you're, well, I hate to say this, Boy Genius, but you're in no shape to fight."

"I can't just sit here and do nothing."

"Let the law handle him then."

"You wouldn't say that if it were your parents who were killed."

Abraham stared at me, then sighed. "Fine, Boy Genius. Have it your way. Go after Rex. No matter how long it takes. But I ask you this: Will it bring back your parents? Will it change anything?"

"They died because of me."

"Listen, Boy Genius. People live and people die. That's the law of nature. Take it from me. In the grand scheme of things, death isn't a big deal. I know that sounds harsh, but it's the truth. In Vietnam, death was all around us. It was just another ordinary event, almost as insignificant as passing gas. Lots of children just like you were orphaned there. They used to line the roads and gather around us with their hands stretched out, begging for a stick of gum. You think those kids dwelled on death? Over there, I used to think long and hard about death. You could say I was obsessed with it. I wondered why we were fighting and dying while rich college kids were back home screwing our sisters and girlfriends. But you know what? I came to realize that it didn't matter. I had to treat death the way the Vietnamese did. If I learned anything from my stint in Vietnam and the Vietnamese people, I learned that. Forget about Rex. His kind will end up dead in some back alley in Guadalajara. You can bet on that. In the meantime, the best thing for you is to stay strong and do what you're best at. I heard that you used to be a genius back where you're from. Who says you can't be a genius again?"

"Who told you that?"

"You've been given a gift, Boy Genius. Don't flush it all away because of this. Man, if I had even a tenth of your brain power, I'd be somebody now and not a joke who's drinking his life away."

"You're not a joke, Abraham."

"It's nice of you to say that, but we both know the truth, don't we? Except for having served my country in the jungles of Southeast Asia and killing a dozen Viet Congs, I've wasted my life, Boy Genius. I drink to try to forget that, but I know the score. My life's been a complete waste and yours will be too if you do what your heart tells you. You've been given a gift. Don't let Rex take that away from you. You're better than that."

A rustling from the edge of the field startled us. I looked up and saw Napalm walking toward us. He was holding a bouquet of yellow lilies. He set the bouquet in front of the wooden cross, then came over to me. "I always knew you ran with a tough crowd, Boy Genius, but who knew they were capable of this? I'm sorry, but you must be strong. If not for yourself, then for the memory of your dear parents. It's what they would have wanted from you, son."

I said nothing. A part of me wanted to tear Napalm's head off. Another part wanted to hug him. So much had changed since my days as a wild dog. But nothing I could do would alter the fact that I was standing next to two crackers and finding comfort in their presence.

A drop of rain hit the tip of my nose. I looked up. A black cloud that looked just like His Excellency the Most Honorable President Park smiled down at me. There was no trace of mockery in His smile. In the distance, a dog howled, *"Traitors must die!"*

CHAPTER 25
Family Reunion

A few days after the funeral, Abraham disappeared from Bogota without a trace. I was sad that he'd left without saying goodbye, but I knew that he must have had his reasons. He was, after all, a Vietnam vet, and his thought processes were a mystery to me. All I knew was that I owed him. He had consoled me through a difficult time, and aside from Rex and the wild dogs, he'd been my oldest friend in Bogota.

Suddenly alone, without family, friends, or wild dogs, Bogota ceased to captivate me. It was no longer the magical haven for dissidents and misfits; and for the first time, I saw it for what it truly was, just another slum devoid of hope or possibility, a breeding ground for tuberculosis and other Third World diseases. Everything about Bogota—strange smells, foreign mutterings, and ill-mannered immigrant children with long immigrant names—repulsed me. I also began to loathe my own skin color, the shape of my eyes, and my very being. I avoided mirrors and pulled constantly at the bridge of my nose, hoping that my flat Mongoloid nose would suddenly turn aquiline. I peroxided my hair blond and purchased light blue contacts. I taped my eyes at night so that the folds would stretch and my eyes would grow larger, making me look more like a Slav or a Swede or even just a dirty wop from the North African island of Sicily, instead of the son of the Orient that I was.

In place of my mother tongue, a combination of primitive grunts and noises always uttered while bowing or wading through rice paddies, I studied French with Ms. Sommers. It was the language of literature, philosophy, and love, a language that had given birth to Camus, Sartre, and de Beauvoir, a language that had forged an empire out of Africa, the Americas, and Indochina, and a language that reeked of rubber plantations and sexy boudoirs and *menage-à-trois's* and *voulez-vous-coucher-avec-moi's*. A language that was self-evidently superior to the language of my forefathers, who had all been ugly little peasants with black teeth who didn't even know how to write their own names and who pulled out their rice dicks only to pee and to produce more peasant babies and who never went down on anyone, and more importantly, who never had anyone go down on them.

"*Bonjour, classe,*" Ms. Sommers called out from the front of the room.

"*Bonjour, Madame,*" I shouted at the top of my lungs.

"*Repondez à moi, classe.*"

"*Oui, madame.*"

"*Vous-êtes Chinois, n'est-ce pas?*"

"*Non, Madame. Je ne suis pas Chinois.*"

"*Vous-êtes jaunes, n'est-ce pas?*"

"*Non, Madame. Je ne suis pas jaune.*"

"*Très bien, classe. Très bien.*"

"*Qu'est-ce que tu veux,* Boy Genius?"

"*Je voudrais tuer les Chinois, Madame. Je voudrais coucher avec vous et toutes les femmes de France.*"

"*Très bien,* Boy Genius. *Très, très bien.*"

BOOK III
Sea of Congee

CHAPTER 26
Summa Cum Ramen

On a crisp spring morning, exactly ten years after I signed the Bogota Accords, I graduated from P.S. 38 with the Ronald Reagan Medal of Honor. This most cherished accolade singled me out as the most promising member of my graduating class and placed me alongside an impressive group of past recipients that included three descendants of the Mayflower and a niece of a U.S. Senator. All had attended P.S. 38 a hundred years earlier, before the influx of illiterate peasants from the Third World.

Holding the medal proudly in my hands, I stood at the dais and thanked everyone who had made my new life possible: Napalm, Ms. Sommers, and Abraham Tomic, all kind white people who, despite my outbursts of anger that stemmed from a poverty-stricken upbringing and other extenuating circumstances, had seen in me a diamond in the rough.

Armed with my degree, my medal, and letters of recommendation from Napalm and Ms. Sommers, I set out for the West Coast in a '64 Galaxie 500 that Ms. Sommers had given me as a graduation gift. I was not sad to leave the East Coast behind. I had grown weary of the city for the usual reasons: rats, roaches, and crime. But more urgent was my desire to get as far away as possible from Bogota's large Puerto Rican population, who gathered nightly on the sidewalk with rickety folding tables for marathon games of Caribbean dominoes while their ever-multiplying litter of unruly children ran about naked, splashing one another with rancid water flowing along the gutters to the city's vast sewer system.

As I drove across the Mississippi and the Great Plains, the same mixture of eager anticipation and visions of striking gold that a thousand Chinamen before me had felt came over me. Then, from the heights of the Rockies, I descended on the majestic waves of the Pacific Ocean just as the sun dipped into the sea.

Standing on a cliff, staring at this magnificent sight and the glistening waters that had once captivated Magellan, I understood why so many coolies had risked so much to come to Gold Mountain throughout history.

I looked up and stared at the sky. There were no clouds or stars that looked like His Excellency. I knew then that the West Coast was truly the land of possibilities.

Within a week of becoming a citizen of the Golden State, I found a job at Peace Now, a small consulting firm that worked to guard corporations against theft. It was the ideal opportunity to utilize my talents and draw from my unique experiences. After having suffered because of His Excellency's whim, I knew firsthand how devastating it was to unjustly lose everything one had worked for overnight.

Peace Now was headquartered in a shiny silver building shaped like a sleek mobile phone in the heart of L.A.'s financial district. Jack Carter, Peace Now's founder and CEO, had commissioned the design from an up-and-coming Boston architect who had apprenticed with the great I.M. Yoo.

I was one of Peace Now's twelve associates. We were all runaways from major East Coast cities; and with the exception of two white women, we were all representatives of minority racial groups and/or members of the homosexual underclass. It was our job to work directly with clients to make sure that the government didn't steal from them.

My first assignment was to help extricate Calvin Dawson, the owner of a microbrewery in Denver, from a legal quagmire. He was facing a discrimination suit from an employee named Janet Cumberland, an African-American who had worked the assembly line at Mr. Dawson's plant for thirteen years. A habitual liar, Janet Cumberland claimed that Mr. Dawson routinely called her a "lazy no-good black bitch" in front of other workers and unfairly passed her over for promotions.

A stocky white man with a barrel chest and a military air about him, Calvin Dawson strutted into Peace Now's main conference room for the initial consultation and shouted, "I didn't promote that lazy no-good black bitch because she was dumb and incompetent, not because she's black!"

"We understand, sir," I said, trying to calm him down.

He slammed his palms on the top of the conference table. "It's blackmail, I tell you. Simple good-old-fashioned blackmail. But what these bastards don't realize is that they don't have a Chinaman's chance of taking my money. You hear me!"

"We'll do everything we can to make sure of that, Mr. Dawson," I said.

He jumped out of his chair and began pacing the room. "My god, I was practically raised by a black woman. Mama Lela, God rest her soul, was as black as they come. Used to feed me and wipe my bottom. My grandfather built that business out of nothing, and there's no way in hell I'm gonna let it all go down the drain 'cuz some lazy no-good black bitch wants to shuffle papers instead of putting in an honest day's work."

"Mr. Dawson, we suggest having four African-Americans, two female and two male, a Chicano and an Asian-American, both females, testify on your behalf so that no one can accuse you of being a racist or a sexist. We'll squash those lines of attack before they can even come up."

He stared at me intently for a moment then said, "You are good at this, aren't you, boy?"

"That goes without saying, Mr. Dawson. We're professionals."

"Right. Of course you are." He guffawed and slapped me on the shoulder.

I can't say I was very fond of Mr. Dawson, but it wasn't my job to make friends with Peace Now's clients. I simply had to make sure they got to hold on to the millions they had earned with hard work and ingenuity.

In court, our character witness, Lakeesha Mogley, an African-American single mother who worked with Peace Now as an independent contractor, testified, "Mr. Dawson is an upstanding model citizen whose consciousness has been enlightened by the Civil Rights Movement. Mr. Dawson has treated me fairly in every way and I've never heard him say anything that even remotely might be construed as supporting the detestable notion that whites are better and more important than nonwhites. Mr. Dawson saw us as people first and foremost. He treats everyone as individuals. I don't think he's even aware that we're a different color. And he's never called me a lazy no-good black bitch."

Another witness, a hard-working African-American named Buck Williams, recalled, "I can't even count up all the times Mr. Dawson's spoken in praise of the noble struggle of Dr. Martin Luther King Jr. Mr. Dawson's said on repeated occasions that Dr. King was a hero to everyone the world over, no matter what their skin color."

Our third witness, Doris Foo, a third-generation Chinese-American from San Francisco's Chinatown, was our ace-in-the-hole. She was a direct descendant of enterprising Chinamen who'd mined for gold with the 49ers and tunneled through the Rockies. Doris had lost three brothers and two uncles to the notorious Chinatown tongs and had had to stand helplessly by as opium took the life of her four sisters and twelve aunts. She took the stand, and in true Oriental fashion, she gritted and recalled, "Ah-ya! Mr. Dawson take my two boy to baseball game. It first time my two boy ever see real stadium. If not for Mr. Dawson, my two boy join Fu Ching or Green Dragon gang and smoke opium and get bullet kill by police. Ah-ya! Mr. Dawson best man in America. He deserving purple heart and medal of honor." She then broke into tears. Three members of the jury cried with her.

In the end, Mr. Dawson was cleared of all charges, and the judge commended him for being a protector of all that the proud Founding Fathers had held dear. As I stared at the faces of Calvin Dawson and my Peace Now colleagues, a surge of satisfaction swelled up from within. I had helped to insure that honest hardworking people would be allowed to keep what they had earned.

As Peace Now thrived, I was awarded several promotions and accompanying raises. I invested wisely and saw my bank account swell. Despite these signs of success, I wasn't happy. I knew that I would eventually hit a glass ceiling because of my appearance. No one, especially not Jack Carter, would admit that such a ceiling existed, but I wasn't blind or stupid. There were only a handful of Chinamen who were successful in U.S. companies; and with the exception of a most super-clever computer maker, every single one owed his success to clandestine backroom deals cut with the CIA.

I had no such deal in place. Now that His Excellency was dead, no one was interested in my stories. The only way I'd ever be CEO of Peace Now was to trick Jack Carter into adopting me. This fact didn't make me bitter. I knew that the decision to prevent me from becoming CEO of Peace Now wasn't personal. It was all a matter of business efficacy. As things were, it was better for Peace Now to have a face like Jack's represent it. Were my face representing Peace Now, clients might mistake it for a Chinese restaurant.

Apart from my professional frustrations, I had yet another problem, which was, in many ways, more urgent and distressing than any glass ceiling. Thanks to Mordechai's cousins who ran the movie industry, the city was teeming with beautiful women— busty blondes, seductive redheads, lithe Filipinas, and spicy Latinas—yet I couldn't get any of them to do unspeakably kinky things to me. No matter how successful I was as a business consultant and a guarantor of their social conscience, beautiful women still eyed me with scorn or nonchalance and reminded me that I was inadequate.

All my problems arose from one source. No matter how many treaties I signed, how diligently I worked, or how much I yearned to belong to my adopted home and live as a true American, the physical features that I'd inherited from my Third World parents marked me as a foreigner. It mattered little that I paid my taxes, regularly made disparaging comments about lazy inner-city youths, and voted with the silent majority. As long as I looked like a relative of Mao Tse Tung, I would forever be viewed with scorn and suspected of being a communist spy. This indelible truth was brought home every time a random child accosted me in the supermarket and said, waving an extended forefinger at me, "Look, a Chinese!"

With effort, an illiterate gypsy goatherd from the Balkans could blend into American life in three years. But as long as my children and their children looked like Uncle Mao, angelic seven-year-olds born to former gypsy goatherds would come up to them and shout, with righteous indignation, "Go back to where you came from!"

To right this injustice, I combed through medical journals in the hope that science had progressed in the direction that Choco Joe had predicted more than a decade earlier. But the only break-throughs I came across were concerned with reviving the sex drives of wealthy old men, and I had no choice but to conclude that Western medicine wasn't willing to help a yellow man fulfill his dream.

Unwilling to kowtow to the conspiracy of Occidental science, I gritted my teeth and placed my hopes on the ancient and secret wisdoms of the Orient. It was, in many ways, an act of despera-tion, but I had little choice. I wasn't prepared to accept the alter-native. I didn't want to die a Chinaman in America.

CHAPTER 27
Tongs and Fireworks

The skinny Nihonjin concierge at the Enola Gay, a four-star hotel in Hiroshima, stared at me with an inscrutable smile when I asked him if he knew of a procedure that could turn Asiatics into handsome Nordics.

"I so sorry, Genius-san. But Japanese science no yet have cure for Middle Kingdom Syndrome," he said.

"Middle Kingdom Syndrome?" It was the first time I'd heard such a fitting label for my condition.

He nodded once and described the symptoms for me. "No have big behind. No have very much facial hair. No have double fold over eye. No like spending money. No muscle tone. No have girlfriend. These all symptom for Middle Kingdom Syndrome. Very very contagious disease. Spread by sexual intercourse. More than one billion people in China suffering from Middle Kingdom Syndrome right now."

It wasn't what I wanted to hear. I took out a hundred-dollar bill and waved it in front of him, then asked him again if he knew of a clinic that could help me.

His eyes opened wide for an instant. "My memory getting little better, Genius-san. Maybe there is cure for Middle Kingdom Syndrome after all."

"Where?"

He snatched the bill from me and said, "Wait here, please." He ducked under the counter, sprung back up, and handed me a small business card. The card was like none I had ever seen before. On it was a picture of a tiny poodle over which was printed in blue, "Namumanu." There was no address and no phone number.

"What am I supposed to do with this?" I asked.

He pointed to the exit and said, in true Zen fashion, "Go across street and follow road one kilometer. There, you see big pachinko parlor name Samurai. Show name card to pachinko man. Pachinko man very friendly. He help you, Genius-san."

I stepped outside and started walking. It was humid out, but not unbearably so. Contrary to my expectations, the air didn't smell of California rolls.

An ambulance raced past with its siren blaring. A dozen schoolchildren in neat black uniforms walked in single file, carrying heavy leather satchels. At a small bridge that crossed a stream, a handful of tourists fed pellets to colorful koi fish.

A kilometer down the road, I reached the Samurai. There were 200 noisy pachinko machines with their accompanying flashing lights. In front of every machine there was a chain-smoking loser who reeked of desperation. I looked around the parlor to see if I could locate someone who was working there. There was no one.

To pass the time, I sat down in front of a machine and began playing. Once I pulled the lever, tiny silver balls rattled down from the top of the machine and raced to the bottom. For some reason, my thoughts turned to my relatives in Seoul. Mother had made a point to send Christmas cards to all her sisters and call her father on Chinese New Year's, but all that had ended with Mother and Father's senseless deaths. Since their passing, I had lost all contact with my clan. I had forgotten what they looked like and only vaguely remembered the face of my dead aunt. As for Mother's father, I had no way of knowing whether he was still alive. The last time I'd spoken to him over the phone, he'd asked me to send him a Walkman, but I'd sent him nothing. It was all for the best, I thought. There would be no more desperate letters from the Hermit Kingdom asking for money for the hundreds of emergencies that befell the average South Korean family year after year. There would be no more requests for blue jeans or fresh American coffee. Once I was cured of Middle Kingdom Syndrome, the members of Mother's clan and I would become complete strangers. Then, were our paths ever to cross, we would walk right past each other without guilt or compunction. I would be freed once and for all from the accident of history that connected me to the mountainous peninsula that jutted out from the rest of Asia like a cancer.

After blowing sixty bucks on pachinko, I stepped away from the machine and searched again for an employee. A wizened old man with a shiny bald pate was sitting on a cheap metal folding chair next to the exit. He had on a thin white undershirt and was fanning himself with a cheap homemade paper fan. I walked over to him and showed him the card that the concierge had given me. He glanced at it for a moment and stared at me blankly.

I explained where I had gotten the card, then said, "Do you know Namu-manu?"

He nodded and pointed at the pachinko machines. "Make money pachinko. Make money pachinko."

It was clear we wouldn't be able to bridge the language barrier. Aggravated, I left the Samurai and walked aimlessly down the street. A dozen Chinese street-portrait painters urged passersby to stop and get their faces enshrined. I fought off their desperate entreaties and continued on, thereby denying six hungry families in the Chinese city of Wuzhou meals for three weeks.

Disgusted with myself for having traveled halfway around the world only to find out that I didn't have a Chinaman's chance of shedding my skin or changing my fate, I ducked into a bar and poured two large bottles of sake into my liver. I didn't particularly enjoy the taste of this hoi polloi rice-paddy beverage, but that wasn't important. What mattered was that it helped me to forget the miserable effects of Middle Kingdom Syndrome for at least a few hours.

I stepped back out onto the street and staggered into a cab. The cabbie took one look at me and said, in perfect English, "Where to, sailor?"

I attributed his calling me a sailor to a local backward custom, and said, "The Enola Gay."

We began moving. Outside, colorful neon lights blurred past the window. In a bin attached to the back of the front seat, there were slick brochures set aside for tourists. All advertised massage parlors and fancy sushi restaurants, but there was no mention of a medical clinic where a miracle operation was being performed.

Suddenly, the neon lights disappeared and we were on a quiet rural road. The taxi shook violently as we traveled over bumps and craters. All around us were perfectly rectangular rice paddies.

"I said I want to go to the Enola Gay!" I shouted.

"Easy there, sailor. This is a shortcut," the cabbie shot back.

It was clear he was trying to take advantage of an inebriated tourist, but I was too tired to complain.

An hour later, we pulled up in front of a drab concrete building in the middle of a vast rice paddy.

"What's this?" I said.

He got out of the cab and opened the door for me. "Dr. Namumanu will take care of you now. You don't have to worry about a thing."

"How did you . . . ?"

"Don't worry about that now. You're late for your appointment."

I stepped out and sauntered toward the building in front of me. It was just a concrete box with a yellow metal door. There were no windows and no signs of any kind. I tried the door. It opened into a spacious lobby filled with a dozen shiny vintage Harleys.

As I stood admiring this amazing collection, a young white woman in a bright white nurse's uniform with strawberry blond hair and milky green eyes came up to me. She smiled and said, in perfect English, "You must be Mr. Boy Genius. The concierge at the Enola Gay told us you'd be coming. Dr. Namumanu will be with you shortly. Please take a seat."

She pointed me to a set of chairs in a small waiting room that looked like it belonged in some cheap Bogota brothel. I half expected to see a room full of Third World sex slaves in cheap negligees.

A tall black man with dreadlocks who reeked of incense was sitting next to me. He grinned and said, "You know, Mr. Chin, I've been waiting for this my whole life, ever since I was a boy in Kingston."

Although my last name wasn't Chin, my keen streetsmarts told me that he was talking to me. I nodded politely and pretended to read a magazine, but he wouldn't let up.

"Hiroshima's a wondrous place, isn't it? It's a terrible shame that we had to drop a bomb here back in the day. But I suppose such tragedy is the price of peace, right? Do you know that the Japanese are the only people in the world who oppose using military force even if their country is invaded? It's true. Researchers surveyed 2,000 Japanese. More than fifty-five percent of them said they were opposed to the use of their own military even if Japan were invaded. If ever there was a country ripe for invading, this would be it. Costa Rica would also be easy to invade, but most people would agree that Japan has more intrinsic value. Don't you think so, Mr. Chin?"

I didn't say anything, but he went on, as if talking was the only way he could keep calm. "The procedure is going to take a little longer for me than it will for you. I've got a little more melanin."

He stopped to laugh nervously, then continued, "It's a dream come true for me, really. And Dr. Namumanu's reputation's just stellar. I personally know two-dozen people who've been to see her, and the results are just spectacular. The power of modern science is mind-boggling, isn't it? And to think, some people still believe that Japan is only good at making those miniature radios!"

I nodded politely. The nurse returned and said, "Mr. Genius, Dr. Namumanu will see you now."

As I got up to follow her, the Rastaman shouted, "Good luck, Mr. Chin!"

The nurse led me up an escalator to a tiny room with a table and a doctor's scale. She told me to sit on the table and then left the room. Restless, I weighed myself and studied the framed certificate that was hanging on the wall. It was from a school I'd never heard of called Chen Zhien Institute of Technology.

Five minutes later, a short Asian woman with shiny silver hooks for arms waddled inside. In the crook of her arm, she was cradling a small gray poodle. Immediately, the poodle began barking at me.

"Calm down, Dr. Kyoko," the woman whispered softly, as she ran her hook over the dog's back. "This famous client from America. You no should have barking like that."

The dog kept barking. Finally, the woman shrugged to signal her surrender, then extended a hook to me and said, "Dr. Namumanu very happy to meet you. This gonna be thousandth time Dr. Namumanu do this operation, so you no worry about nothing."

I shook her hook and managed a feeble smile.

"Before Dr. Namumanu go on, how you gonna pay for the procedure?"

I took out my wallet and handed her a credit card. She held the card up to a security camera in the ceiling, then handed it back to me. "Very good. We ready to rock and roll. Now shirt please."

"Excuse me?"

"Dr. Namumanu say shirt now please."

"I don't understand."

She waved one hook in front of me angrily. "Dr. Namumanu say take your shirt off."

I nodded and unbuttoned my shirt. Dr. Namumanu's poodle growled at me again.

Dr. Namumanu snatched the shirt from me and stared at my back. "Why you have funny writing on your back?"

"It's just a birth defect," I said.

She made a strange face, then threw my shirt to the far corner of the room. "Now lie on table."

I did as I was told. The table was covered with a thin sheet of clear plastic, and it quickly stuck to my back. On the ceiling, there was a black-and-white checkerboard pattern. Staring at it, I was reminded of the grueling chess games that Choco Joe and I had played at KBS. I wondered where Choco Joe was and how he'd fared since His Excellency's death.

Dr. Namumanu poked my chest with her metal hook, all the while cradling her dog in her other arm. After several pokes, she said, "How you feeling these days?"

"Pretty good, Doctor," I said nervously.

She poked my ribs. "Any pain?"

"No."

She pressed her metal hook just below my navel. "Eating good?"

"Sure," I said.

She pulled her metal hook off me and said, "You have very good spleen. Very good spleen. Excellent spleen."

"Excuse me?"

"Dr. Namumanu give you compliment. Your spleen in excellent condition."

That did it. I sat up and said, "Doctor, about this operation . . . "

She stared at me a while then cackled. "No worry about a thing. Dr. Namumanu gonna take good care of you, Good Spleen Man. Dr. Namumanu no gonna even cut you or open you up. Entire procedure done with acupuncture and Chinese medicine. Everything hundred cent organic. So no worry 'bout nothing and lie down."

I just sat there, trying to decide what I ought to do.

The door creaked open, and a nurse who looked like all the rest walked in. Unlike the earlier nurse, her smell was intoxicating, though I couldn't quite figure out what it was.

She held up a syringe and said, "My name's Nurse Five. I'll be assisting Dr. Namumanu today." Her voice was soft and gentle like that of a familiar chanteuse.

Before I could respond, she grabbed my wrist and inserted the needle into a vein in my forearm. Dr. Namumanu grinned like an idiot, and her dog growled more loudly than before. The doctor shook her head and said, "You have too much fear, Good Spleen Man. Fear very bad for spleen."

Nurse Five flicked a switch on the wall. Instantly, the room went dark and the sound of waves filled my ears. I felt faint.

"May I have some water?" I shouted into the darkness.

Dr. Namumanu cackled. A hand undid my belt and tugged at my pants. Cold metal touched my thighs and I blacked out.

CHAPTER 28

Dreaming of Reunification

The first thing I saw when I came to was the outline of Nurse Five's full breasts pressing out against her dress.

"How do you feel, Mr. Genius?" she asked.

"What happened?" I said, sitting up slowly. I had no memory at all of the operation.

"Everything went fine. You're good to go."

Behind her, Dr. Namumanu was taking off a pair of black leather gloves. She glanced at me and shouted, "Everything finish, Good Spleen Man. Dr. Namumanu do number-one job on you. You no gonna regret nothing. Everything excellent condition. Like your spleen."

Nurse Five handed me a cup of water. "You'll feel slightly dizzy for a couple of days, but that's only the medication wearing off. After that, you'll feel much better."

I sipped some water, then said, "Can I see a mirror?"

Nurse Five nodded, then held up a small round mirror in front of me. I stared into the metallic surface.

There was no sign of blood or pus. In the mirror, a new man was staring back at me. His face was chiseled, his eyes were blue, his lips were thin, and his nose was aquiline.

I turned to Nurse Five.

"Well, what d'you think?" she asked, smiling calmly.

"I can't believe this," I said, tracing the outline of my nose with my forefinger. "I hoped the results would be good, but this is beyond my wildest expectations. This is amazing."

"You'll get used to it. Everyone does."

Before I could say another word, Dr. Namumanu rushed over

and barked, "Time for you to go, Good Spleen Man. Dr. Namumanu running hospital, not a hotel!"

Nurse Five helped me to my feet, helped me get dressed, then led me gingerly out the door.

From behind us, Dr. Namumanu called out, "Take good care of your spleen, Good Spleen Man! Make sure to get plenty exercise. Exercise very important for spleen!"

I did my best to ignore the doctor's last-minute suggestions, then turned to Nurse Five. "Thank you."

She stared at me for a long while then put a hand on my cheek. "Don't thank me, thank Dr. Namumanu. She's not just a doctor, she's an artist."

I took one last look at Dr. Namumanu's clinic. It was true. Dr. Namumanu had performed a miracle and made me a new man.

CHAPTER 29
Thriller in the Jungle

My new face opened up a new world to me. No one ever stopped to ask me where I was from. No one felt compelled to comment on how great my English was. No former goatherd or penniless Puerto Rican dared to address me as an equal or an inferior. And no spoiled brat ever ran up to me to shout, "Chinese!" In short, for the first time in my life, I felt at home in America.

The Peace Now staff was baffled by my transformation. At our weekly staff meeting, Jack Carter stared at me quizzically and said, "Did you get a new haircut, Boy Genius?"

"No, sir," I said.

"A new suit?"

"No, sir."

He rubbed his chin and furrowed his brow. "You've started working out then?"

"No, sir."

"Whatever you're doing, keep it up. Business has never been better. Everyone's saying glowing things about you. You're kicking ass."

My colleagues stared at me with envy. I thrust my aquiline nose high in the air and relished my new sense of self. I knew I had arrived, and it was now time for bigger and better things.

Armed with the perfect combination of looks, brains, and talent, I was prepared to do whatever was necessary to attain what my poor parents had always wanted for me, a palatial house with white neighbors.

I left Peace Now and joined an upstart computer software company. My job was to persuade corporations that they needed our services. It wasn't a challenging task, but it was extremely profitable. Most had no idea what I was talking about, but everyone was convinced that the world was undergoing a silent revolution. All I had to do was pepper my sales pitch with catchphrases like "dinosaur" and "next millennium."

When not closing A-list sales, I cruised L.A.'s trendiest bars and nightclubs. For the first time in my life, I experienced what it was to be the object of desire. As soon I set foot in a room, a dozen women stopped what they were doing and sent me psychic messages begging me to talk to them.

My first conquest was a nameless, faceless daughter of the Midwest who agreed to come home with me after just two drinks.

"Come in my mouth," she whispered in a gravelly voice that she'd learned from the movies, as she peered up at me with eyes the color of the Minnesota sky. Her curly blond hair smelled like waffles and her soft full breasts rubbed against the front of my thighs. I obliged and shot two cups of yellow semen deep into her esophagus. Through it all, she had no clue that she'd just swallowed an army of yellow children and the blood coursing through the mound of white flesh inside her mouth was that of a yellow cur born of centuries of coolie labor.

Later that night, I christened my penis Jesus (Hay-soos) in honor of the Jewish prophet whose teachings had meant so much to Mother. In the months that followed, I rammed Jesus into every lonely white young woman who'd migrated to L.A. for a shot at stardom. The faces of these women barely registered. All I remembered was the color of their hair. Blond, brunette, or strawberry red. Each woman I defiled was a band-aid for every slight, snub, and indignation I had suffered as a Chinese coolie in America. Each woman I defiled was a trophy for Jesus.

But even the intense pleasure I'd initially found in unmentionable acts with nameless women soon ebbed away, leaving me with the same hollowness that had always gnawed at me.

It was then that I received an invitation to Namumanu III, the party to celebrate the opening of Dr. Namumanu's first clinic in North America.

"Giving home to homeless very cruel, Good Spleen Man. It taking away identity. Making them invisible. They no longer homeless so what they gonna do?" Dr. Namumanu explained, as she welcomed me inside the large dancehall, a former homeless shelter that Mordechai's third son had converted into a trendy discotheque.

I just nodded. One of my past incarnations might have tried futilely to argue with Dr. Namumanu's unique brand of logic, but I didn't care anymore. Homelessness, disease, old age, and other such unpleasant Third World concepts were no longer a part of my reality. I was no longer allied with losers whose only chance of buying their way out of slavery was to pick six correct numbers in the lottery.

There were more than 200 people milling about and dancing to the ever-festive tunes of a live mariachi band. I was wandering around and admiring Dr. Namumanu's craftsmanship when I spotted Nurse Five standing in a corner. She was wearing a stunning red dress that showed off her long legs and ample bosom.

I walked over to her and said, "You look fabulous, Nurse Five."

She blushed slightly and said, "Please, call me Rosalyn."

"It's good to see you again, Rosalyn."

"It's good to see you too."

A wiry old Filipino whose skin was leathery like a baseball glove from the last century walked past holding a tray of drinks. Rosalyn deftly snagged two glasses and handed me one.

"I hope you like ice wine," she said.

"It's my favorite," I replied, then clinked glasses.

After a few sips, she said, "I have a confession to make." Her tone was intriguing and seductive. I was completely sucked in.

"What's the confession?"

She smiled. "I know who you are." She spoke as if she were letting me in on a secret on which the fate of the world depended.

"Sure you do. You saw me before the operation."

"No, I mean from a long time ago, when you were a boy."

I studied her face and tried unsuccessfully to place her in my past. "I'm sorry, but I just can't seem to recall where we might have met. Are you sure we've met? I think I would remember your eyes. They're remarkable," I said, trying my best to sound sincere.

"Oh, you're just saying that. Anyway, think hard now. I'll give you a clue. It was during your childhood. You were the biggest bad-ass in school."

"Bad-ass?"

"You really don't know?" she said, tilting her head to one side.

"I haven't a clue."

"I used to be a bit shorter." She then bent down and stared up at me. Stooped like that, she looked strangely familiar. "Here's a final clue, Boy Genius. You couldn't stand me back then, and I'm afraid I was unjustly mean to you."

I tried to recall those who had been unjustly mean to me from my childhood. The list began with His Excellency and went on and on.

Finally, Nurse Five said, "It's me, Boy Genius. Judy Kim. From P.S. 38."

I nearly fell over from the shock. "Judy Kim? But how could that be? You must be a foot taller now."

"A foot and a half. What can I say? Dr. Namumanu works miracles. I was such a shrimp back then. The world really does look a lot better from up here. I hope you're not still mad at me, Boy Genius."

"Mad at you? Why should I be mad at you?"

"I was somewhat critical of you back then. Had to compensate for, well, you know. But that's the old Judy Kim. I'm Rosalyn Waters now and I think far better for it. But you have to admit you were partly to blame. You were such a troublemaker. You had such a problem with authority. Had the biggest chip on your shoulder. We're talking major, major attitude problem. You wouldn't let poor Ms. Sommers alone. Day after day with your impromptu history lessons. The poor woman. It's amazing you didn't give her a heart attack. Do you remember Principal Napalm?"

"I haven't seen him in a couple of years now."

"Did you know that he had a nervous breakdown soon after we graduated? They called it early retirement, but the truth is he just went loony."

"I didn't know that," I said.

"Can't blame him, can you? That neighborhood was so bad. Can you believe we actually survived that place? Fights every day and kids with butterfly knives. If you think about it, you and I both survived deprived childhoods."

"Right."

She brightened up. "How do you like your new face, by the way?"

"It takes a little getting used to, but I can't complain. The people who knew me before were completely baffled though."

"Don't tell me. They knew something was different, but they couldn't quite put their fingers on it."

"Exactly," I said.

"Same thing happened to me when I got the procedure done. People will be confused like that for about six months. Then, they'll forget who you were in the past. People I meet now just assume I'm from Estonia or the Ukraine. It's all thanks to Dr. Namumanu. She's the most brilliant person I've ever met. I hate to throw the word around, but she's a genius. That's the only way to describe it."

"How'd you meet up with her?" I was genuinely curious.

"The same way everyone does, I guess. You find her if you look for her hard enough. She doesn't advertise, you know. Doesn't have to. People just show up at her doorstep from all over the world. Just last week, she performed the procedure on an eighty-year-old woman from Bolivia. The woman had saved her entire life so she could get the face of the Queen of England."

"Did she get it?"

"Of course. Dr. Namumanu can do miracles. She's made so many breakthroughs. Do you know that she can now perform the procedure in half an hour?"

"That fast?" I responded.

"She's still not satisfied. She wants to be able to do the procedure in ten minutes or less. She wants to open a chain of clinics all around the world so that people can walk in anytime and walk out with a whole new face. I believe she can do it. She can do anything."

I took a chance and said, "Listen, Rosalyn. How 'bout we slip out and go for a drive. You and I can reminisce some more. What d'you say?"

She glanced quickly at Dr. Namumanu, who was standing across from us, then said, "Okay. Let's go."

We got in my car, a German sedan, and drove south to an empty beach. The full moon shone brightly above us and the breaking surf called out our names. Rosalyn and I sat at the water's edge and stared at the waves.

"Have you ever gone back?" I asked.

"Where?"

"Bogota."

"No, never. The place only holds bad memories for me," she said.

"I understand."

"Have you?"

"Have I what?"

"Have you ever gone back there?" she asked.

"No."

We said nothing for a long while. Then, Rosalyn drew a circle in the sand with her finger. "I'm sorry about your parents. I wanted to tell you that when we were kids, but something always kept me from telling you. To this day I'm not sure what."

"Forget it. It's all in the past. Anyway, it's not something I like to talk about."

"My parents died too. It happened when I was in college.

They were driving up to see me but they never made it. A truck hit them head-on. They died instantly."

"I'm sorry."

"It's not your fault. It upset me quite a bit when it happened, but I'm over it now. It's not a big deal really. They were around before. Now they're not. Things like that happen, and there's nothing we can do."

"Rosalyn?"

She stared at me. The green of her eyes was enchanting. I put a hand on her cheek and kissed her. Her lips were soft and warm.

"Why'd you do that?" she asked, when our lips unlocked.

"You're beautiful," I said, then kissed her again.

In the remaining hours of the night, we made love like two teenagers. When we were done, Rosalyn looked at me with tears in her eyes.

"What's wrong?" I asked.

She turned away from me.

"What's wrong?" I asked again, worried that I had let her down somehow.

She shuddered and said, "I'm so sorry."

"For what?"

"I'm so wrong for you."

"What d'you mean? What are you talking about?"

She sighed and said, "I'll never be a daughter of the Mayflower. I'm so sorry."

I held her close. "It's okay. I won't tell anyone."

CHAPTER 30
Carp and Koi Fish

Six months later, Rosalyn and I were married at a quaint San Mateo monastery that had once been a winery. Dr. Namumanu performed the ceremony. Dr. Kyoko was the flower girl, and nurses from Dr. Namumanu's clinic were bridesmaids.

I'm not sure what it was about Rosalyn that drew me to her. Perhaps it was that we were so very different. She'd never had to wage a secret war against those around her. She'd never been exploited by a charismatic dictator. And she'd never had her own KBS TV show. On the other hand, once we scratched the surface, we weren't very different at all. We'd both grown up in Bogota, and we'd both been driven to reinvent ourselves to survive in the world. Most importantly, we'd both lost our parents and were orphans.

The only member of any clan from the Land of Morning Calm to attend the wedding was Rosalyn's aunt who flew in from Boston's Chinatown. A demure woman whose crooked back, wrinkled face, and blistered fingers attested to many years of hard labor behind a sewing machine, she stared at me with awe when Rosalyn introduced us, then clapped her hands and said, "He lookie like a movie star."

Her inscrutable yellow face made me think about Mother and Father. Their conspicuous absence reminded me yet again of what Rex and the wild dogs had taken from me. But for the first time, I wasn't entirely saddened by this. Had Mother and Father been alive, they would have turned my wedding into a tawdry immigrant affair.

Every green-grocer or laundryman with even remote ties to

Mother and Father's clans, and every smiling Korean they'd ever crossed paths with in America, would have been invited to the wedding out of a perverse Oriental compulsion to save face.

"This right thing to do, Boy Genius," Mother would have said, as she added yet another Lee Park Kim Choi to the guest list. The ceremony would have been conducted by a Korean minister who would no doubt have read endless excerpts aloud from the King James Bible in both Korean and bastardized English. At the reception, Rosalyn and I would have had to make the rounds and bow to a hundred haggard immigrants as we tried our best not to cringe at their cheap Sunday suits and garish dresses. All the while, the hall would have been filled with a never-ending stream of gossip about whose children had made it and whose had not, whose sons were filial and whose were not. When it was all over, a blurb about the union would have appeared in the back pages of the New York and Los Angeles editions of *Korea Today* with accompanying photographs of Rosalyn and me.

As fate would have it, Rex had rescued me from a degrading dog-and-pony show. As soon as Dr. Namumanu pronounced Rosalyn and me husband and wife, we raced to the airport and boarded a plane for Paris.

For the next month, we visited Europe's most precious cities and marveled at all the history that was captured in the walls of every picturesque little village. At a postcard café near the Eiffel Tower, Rosalyn and I promised each other that we would return to Europe every chance we got to get better acquainted with our roots. After all, we might have been Americans, but our forefathers had been Europeans.

When we returned from our honeymoon, Rosalyn and I settled into a pleasant and comfortable routine. Outwardly, we had what many would call an enviable marriage. We remembered each other's birthdays. We made a point to spend at least two nights a week doing something together. We slept in on Sundays and enjoyed long quiet walks on the beach. We scratched each other's backs at night before falling asleep in each other's arms. At times, it irked me that she knew so much about my past. But it also comforted me that she loved me despite it. No one in my new life knew about my association with a gang of murderous wild dogs. As tolerant as people professed to be, I knew that there were always limits.

As for our material well-being, thanks to the boom in the computer industry and the success of Dr. Namumanu's revolutionary procedure, we quickly acquired what my parents had once dreamed of owning: a spacious house with a lovely view, a diligent Mexican cleaning woman, and wealthy white neighbors.

The only thing that was not ideal in my new family—created in order to escape the memory of my old one—was Dr. Namumanu. As great a debt as I owed her, I didn't like her and resented the way she intruded into our life. She routinely showed up at our house at odd hours without ever being invited, and she insisted that we join her for fabulous weekend getaways. It was as if Dr. Namumanu was the officious, overbearing mother-in-law. When I brought this up with Rosalyn, she just said, "She's only trying to help us. I wish you wouldn't be so critical of her. She's a very special person."

So it was that I found myself, on an unusually chilly spring evening that coincided with the fifteenth anniversary of His Excellency's Death, at a movie premiere with Dr. Namumanu and Rosalyn.

The theater was packed with perfect aquiline noses and faces without wrinkles. Whoever had said that the fountain of youth was a chimera was wrong, and the denizens of L.A. were living proof. Money could buy not only fame and love, but it could stave off old age and make sure that adolescence lasted long into one's seventies.

Just when the lights dimmed and the movie, a mindless epic called *American Drifter*, started, Dr. Namumanu put a cold hook on my arm and said, "By the way, Good Spleen Man. Dr. Namumanu want to congratulate you. You gonna be a father soon."

The news startled me. I glanced over at Rosalyn. She saw the question in my face and said, "It's been three months now, honey."

I was piqued that Dr. Namumanu knew about Rosalyn's pregnancy before I did, but I didn't let that get me down. I was going to be a father soon, and Mother and Father's genes wouldn't die with me.

Buoyed by the excitement of this development, I found it difficult to concentrate on the movie, a pathetic little drama about a Comanche warrior who falls in love with a fur trader's daughter. Still, when the film ended, I stood up and clapped for a full minute like everyone else in the room.

Amidst the applause, Dr. Namumanu leaned toward me and said, "You trust Dr. Namumanu, Good Spleen Man. This star of this movie gonna be very big star. He name Clark Klarkson and he go back long time with Dr. Namumanu. He spleen not so good like you, but he still very handsome."

I nodded politely and followed Dr. Namumanu out to the lobby for the requisite post-screening reception. Several up-and-coming young actors were clustered here and there, and Dr. Namumanu seemed to know all of them. I didn't bother to ask her whom she had done the procedure on. After my own experience with her miracle treatment, I wouldn't have batted an eye if it turned out that half of Hollywood's biggest stars were former citizens of the People's Republic.

Since I had nothing to gain from schmoozing with movie people, I drifted off to the makeshift bar in the corner. The same twelve old Filipinos who seemed to work every party were serving drinks and hors d'oeuvres. I grabbed two gin and tonics and a six-pack, and slipped back into the empty theater. Sitting in the very back of the room, I downed both drinks and began to nurse the beers.

"They say that Harry Kellar performed here in the 1920s," a voice said.

I looked up. A thin white man with a rugged jaw and a movie-star dimple in the middle of his chin was smiling at me. He had on movie-star shades that were even larger than the sunglasses His Excellency had worn.

"I hope I didn't startle you," he said. "I just wanted you to know about Harry Kellar."

"Who?"

"Harry Kellar. He was a famous magician and a great friend of Ching Ling Foo." He paused. "You don't know who that is either, do you?"

"I can't say I do."

"Ching Ling Foo was one of the greatest illusionists from the Orient to ever share his magic with the West. In the 1920s, he mystified audiences by catching bullets in his teeth and producing bowls with colorful goldfish swimming in them out of thin air. People who saw him perform swore his magic was superior to all the rest, even Harry Houdini, who some people say was the greatest of all."

I nodded politely.

He stared at me for a while longer, then placed a hand on my shoulder.

I pushed his hand off me and said, "Please don't touch me."

He smiled mischievously. "You're a trip, man. Always were. Always will be."

That's when I recognized him. He was the terrible actor who had starred in *American Drifter*.

"You look great, man. Dr. Namumanu's obviously done a bang-up job on you," he said.

"I think you have me mistaken for someone else."

"Come on, man. Don't be like that. You and I go way back."

"I'm not from here. You have me mistaken for someone else."

"It's no mistake, man. You might look like that on the outside, but I know it's you, Boy Genius."

The sound of my name startled me. "How the hell do you know my name?"

"It's me, man. Your old buddy Rex, from Bogota." He put his hands out and grabbed me by the shoulders.

A shiver ran down my spine. If he really was who he claimed to be, I would finally get my chance at revenge. "Get your dirty paws off me, you dirty dog!" I shouted, pushing his hand away.

"What's your problem, man?"

In lieu of a reply, I punched him square in the face. He fell to the floor, then got up slowly. There was blood oozing out of the corner of his mouth. It was the first time I'd ever drawn blood from Rex. He wiped the blood off his mouth, and said, "What's wrong with you, man? There are people with cameras here."

"You may have been stronger than me when we were kids, but I'm older now. I'm going to kill you whether you fight back or not."

I lunged at him. He jumped back with both grace and power. He hadn't lost his wild dog reflexes at all.

"You haven't figured it out, have you?" he shouted. "Oh, man. This is terrific. The smartest boy in Bogota, and you couldn't figure out what a self-taught mutt could. It was Abraham. We thought he was just a drunk, but he set us up. He's a real ruthless bastard, just like the three thugs who showed up with him that day."

"What three thugs?"

"They came in black suits and sunglasses. We tried to save your crazy parents, but they were too strong for us. I was the only one who managed to escape. But I saw what really went down. I saw it all."

"You're lying."

"Abraham and his three goons killed your parents then made it look like it was me. And you fell for it. One hundred percent. My god. All these years. You must have been . . ."

"Don't lie to me."

"Why would I lie about this stuff? Why would I make this up?"

"Because you're a coward."

He shook his head. "Listen, Boy Genius. You and I go way back, but please be careful what you say. I've done many shameful things in my life, but I am no coward."

"You killed my parents."

"I told you it was Abraham and his goons. I'll prove it to you. One of them had a scar on his face. On his cheek. Some letters. A-B-C or something like that."

I couldn't move. I could hear His Excellency laughing at me from the grave.

"I know what you must be going through, Boy Genius. I wanted to kill Abraham too. I'm sorry."

"What happened that day? Tell me everything."

"Abraham took those three men to your house. Right away, I knew they were up to no good. We wild dogs have a sixth sense about that sort of thing. I rallied the others to help your parents, but they didn't want to help. They were angry about the Bogota Accords. But I reminded them of our duty to be loyal and convinced them to fight. And we did. Every single one of us. But they were too strong, especially the one with the scar. He fought like a machine. When it was all over, I was the only one alive. To this day, I wonder why me? Why was I allowed to live when everyone else was slaughtered? I may look like this on the outside and you may think I'm living it up now as a movie star, but there are still nights when I hear the screams of the old gang. I was their leader, yet I could do nothing to protect them. Most of them were just puppies. Do you know what it's like to have the blood of puppies on your hands? I'm glad you don't. No one deserves such a thing. They were the only family I ever had. I chased the three men as far north as Niagara Falls, but then winter set in and I had to turn back. It wasn't the cold that stopped me. I just didn't have the will to go on. It got to the point where all I wanted to do was lick the insides of beer bottles. By the time I got back to Bogota many years later, Abraham was gone and so were you. You'd abandoned Bogota."

"I didn't abandon Bogota."

"Call it what you want, Boy Genius. I don't want to lay a guilt trip on you or anything, but that shattered me. I never thought you'd do that. Other kids? Maybe. But not you. Not my homeboy. Even when you signed the Bogota Accords, I figured you were pulling some slick con on your teachers. That's what it was, wasn't it?"

"I didn't turn on you. I'm not a traitor."

"I never said you were. Look, forget it. It's all in the past. Bridge under water, as they say. Bridge under water. I'm just telling you how I felt. A part of me wanted to kill you. But then, I told myself that regardless of who was to blame, you'd lost your parents. You'd suffered. I know what that's like. I'm an orphan too, you know. Anyway, I wandered around aimlessly until I ran into Dr. Namumanu. And everything since then is what they call cinema history."

"You know Dr. Namumanu?"

"Sure, she and I go way back. Man, if it weren't for me, you wouldn't have gotten the treatment you got. She tested the procedure on half a dozen lucky dogs before she started working on humans. I was one of the first dogs she ever worked on. And letting her work on me was the best thing I ever did. Before I knew it I was in L.A. and there were posters of me everywhere. But who knows how long all this is going to last, right? As the saying goes, L.A. is like Oz and New York is like Wonderland. In L.A., little men behind curtains fool you with big pictures and in New York, you either feel really big or really small. Anyway, isn't this crazy? Boy Genius and Rex living it up in sunny Southern California. Who would ever believe what we've been through? By the way, I heard about the marriage. Congratulations, man. I envy you. I really do. Nothing in the world can compare to a real family, right?"

My lungs felt like His Excellency was squeezing them. I leaned back against the wall.

"You okay, Boy Genius?"

"You should have told me. You should have told me a long time ago."

"Hey, I wanted to tell you. But you weren't around."

"Where is Abraham now?"

"What good will that do, Boy Genius?"

"Where is he?"

"I don't know. And I don't think I'd tell you even if I did."

"Why not?"

"So much has happened since then, and you and I have both changed. What'd be the point?"

"He killed my parents. He has to pay."

"I don't know where Abraham is. I really don't. All I can say is maybe try the phone book."

I slid down against the wall and sat on the floor.

Rex smiled awkwardly. "Anyway, Boy Genius, I gotta go. It was great seeing you again. I got a movie to shoot in Rome next month, but I'll be in town for another week or so. Give me a call and maybe we can hang."

I didn't say anything. After Rex walked away, I sat there in the empty theater for a long time. Every now and then, the sound of laughter echoed through the walls and made me nauseous. About an hour later, Rosalyn came inside. She touched my face softly and said, "Are you okay, baby?"

"I'm fine."

"I was worried about you. You'd disappeared. I thought maybe you were upset about something." There was genuine concern in her voice, and it warmed me to know that someone actually cared about me.

"I'm sorry. I ran into someone I used to know," I said.

"Oh, you mean Clark."

"Clark?"

"The movie star. Dr. Namumanu introduced us. He told us all about how you two grew up together. I think Dr. Namumanu's right about him. He's going to be a big star. Isn't it exciting?"

The door swung open again and Dr. Namumanu burst inside. "Here you are, Rosalyn. Dr. Namumanu been looking all over for you. Twenty-five people out there want to sign up for Dr. Namumanu operation. Come on. We got lotta work to do."

Rosalyn glanced at me and said, "Let's go back to the reception, honey."

"You go ahead. I'll be out there in a little while."

"You sure you're okay?"

"I'm fine."

She kissed me and smiled, then turned to go with Dr. Namumanu. I glanced at her stomach. I hadn't noticed it earlier, but she was beginning to show. I tried to picture her ballooned out like a Kewpie doll. It suited her well. In six months, if all went well, a tiny yellow baby with an above-average I.Q. would pop out of her. We would name the child something clever and then hire someone to take care of it. Most of our neighbors had Mexican nannies, but Chinese nannies were starting to be fashionable again. The child would grow up comfortable and happy. The child would have everything he or she wanted and never have to spend any time locked up in any basement.

Laughter floated through the walls again. To escape the oppressive gaiety, I slipped quietly outside and began walking aimlessly, placing one foot in front of the other. The air was unusually cold. Along the street, a hundred invisible sprinklers sprayed a fine mist on tall plastic palm trees that had been imported from South America. A sign written in both English and Spanish said the water that was being sprayed had been recycled from the sewer system and warned passersby not to drink it. I didn't care. I stuck my head under the spray and opened my mouth wide.

Across the street, three drunk Mexican men straggled out of a taco truck and began singing loudly in their native tongue. An ambulance raced past with its sirens blaring and bathed me in red light. Somewhere in the city another soul was dying, alone and afraid. Just when I thought I'd put my past behind me, His Excellency had resurfaced and reminded me yet again that my life wasn't really my own.

I waved my fist at the sky and shouted, "Look at what you've done to me, Your Excellency!"

Twenty years had passed since I'd left the Hermit Kingdom, yet I still couldn't speak His Excellency's name without turning into a frightened little boy.

CHAPTER 31
Asexual Reproduction

My relationship with Rosalyn soured after my run-in with Rex, even as her body pushed her ever closer toward motherhood. She accused me of being needlessly moody and pessimistic. I accused her of being a mindless slave to Dr. Namumanu's every whim. Our disagreements were exacerbated by the strains of Rosalyn's pregnancy and the accompanying hormonal changes. Despite knowing all this, I still withheld my sympathy and affection. I knew I was being cruel, but I couldn't help myself. I wanted to lash out against something, and she happened to be nearby.

This tension naturally took its toll on my work. I couldn't concentrate on my clients. My sales plummeted. Still, the industry thrived. Every day, hundreds of people showed up at our company and offered to give us money. People believed in technology and science the way old Puerto Rican women in Bogota believed in saints and miracles.

I didn't believe in saints or miracles. Everyone I had ever put my faith in had turned out to be a liar, and the only two people who had ever been honest with me were gone, murdered by H-I-J. His Excellency may have been dead, but H-I-J and others like him were busy carrying out His orders. I remembered the smile that had graced his grotesque face when he'd interviewed me for my exit visa. I wanted to see him just once more so I could wipe that smile permanently from his face.

The only clue I had to find H-I-J was Abraham Tomic. I'd spent my entire life believing that wild dogs had murdered my parents when the truth was that a homeless Vietnam vet had sold me out to His Excellency's number-one goon. A homeless

Vietnam vet had duped me into believing that becoming a genius again was worth something. A homeless Vietnam vet had turned me into a coward.

Driven by a desperate need to wreak long-overdue revenge, I called my only remaining ally on the East Coast. After I explained what had happened, Ms. Sommers said, "There's not much I can do, Boy Genius. Why don't you try contacting Franklin?"

"Who?"

"I'm sorry, you must have known him as Tanh."

"You mean the refugee boy from Vietnam who endured pirate attacks and starvation to come to America?"

"That's the one. He goes by Franklin now. And he's just been elected mayor of your hometown."

"You're kidding."

"When have you ever known me to kid around, Boy Genius? Franklin's a fine young man and a great politician. He keeps in touch with me. Comes by the house every now and then. He asks about you sometimes, but of course, I never have much to tell him."

"I've been busy. I'm sorry."

"Franklin's busy too. But he makes time. I'm so proud of him. Most people around here didn't think he had much of a chance. He was running against an entrenched incumbent, an old fart, if you ask me. But he campaigned hard and won a lot of people over. I'm happy to say I voted for him. Not enough young people are going into politics these days."

"How do I get in touch with him?"

"Hang on and I'll get his number for you."

I called the number as soon as I got off the phone with Ms. Sommers. Tanh wasn't in, but a smart-sounding secretary who had no trace of a Bogota accent took my message.

Afterwards, I downed two martinis to offset the jolt I'd gotten from the news that someone with an average I.Q. who'd never received the Ronald Reagan Medal of Honor had actually made something of himself. I hadn't expected Tanh to end up incarcerated and/or dead like my other distinguished classmates from P.S. 38, but the most I'd ever envisioned for him was a life hawking knockoff designer watches and bags the way his wiry compatriots seemed to do in every city with a Chinatown.

Tanh returned my call early the next morning.

"Boy Genius, my man. How the hell are you?" he asked crisply, confidently, and with no trace of a Ho Chi Minh accent. Had I not known whom I was speaking to, I might very well have missed the fact that I was talking to a refugee who'd been chased out of his country by communists.

"Tanh?"

"It's Frank now. Frank Uhung, the Second."

"Right, I'm sorry."

"Forget it. It's no big deal. Anyway, it's good to hear your voice, man. How long has it been?"

"It's been a while."

"Bogota's never been the same without you. Why don't you come back? We could always use someone like you here. I don't know if you've heard, but . . ."

"Congratulations on becoming mayor. Ms. Sommers couldn't stop raving about you. It's quite an accomplishment."

"Thanks. The way I see it, I had no choice. Stepping into the ring is the only way to make sure the system works the way it should, right?"

"You must have had one hell of a campaign."

"It was something. Most people didn't think I had a chance. And to be honest with you, I couldn't blame them. The demographic here says, no way I should have won."

"Then how'd you do it?"

"A lot of it was luck. The Dominicans were fighting the Mexicans. The Mexicans were fighting the Colombians. I stepped in and won the Puerto Rican swing vote."

"How?"

"My wife is Chinese-Cuban. Chino-Cubano, as they say."

"That's all it took?"

"I also promised them a parade. I don't know if you know this, Boy Genius, but people from the Caribbean are extremely partial to parades. Anyway, enough talk of politics, what can I do you for?"

"I'm looking for someone."

"Enough said. I won't pry into the details. Just tell me one thing. Is it anyone I know?"

"I don't think so."

When I finished explaining my situation, he was quiet for a while, then said, "Listen, Boy Genius. I can't make any guarantees, but I'll see what I can do."

"Thanks, Frank. I really appreciate this."

"Don't mention it. Just remember, Frank Uhung never forgets a friend."

I thanked him and hung up. The more I thought about it, the more I couldn't help but marvel at Tanh's achievement. He'd reinvented himself completely while remaining in Bogota. Either he was incredibly resourceful or whatever information he'd passed on to the CIA in order to gain his post must have been extremely valuable.

Two days later, a package arrived at my doorstep. Inside, there was a thick manila folder and a note that said, *"Knowledge is power and information is the only thing we really have on anyone. —F.U. II"*

Inside the folder, there were a dozen photographs of Abraham and a thick stack of documents. According to them, Abraham Tomic had been born in 1956 to a prominent Chicago family. His grandfather had been governor of Illinois during the Depression, and his father had been an economics professor at the University of Chicago. Abraham had attended the University of Chicago but dropped out two months prior to graduation. For the next fifteen years, he traveled throughout Central and South America, developing an addiction to cocaine and various other illicit substances. He returned to the U.S. in the early 1980s and settled in Bogota. According to Bogota police records, he'd been rounded up more than two dozen times for disorderly conduct and possession of narcotics. Despite these many run-ins with the law, he'd never served any jail time. I could only guess that some-one from his family had intervened on his behalf. Strangely, there was no mention anywhere of Abraham ever having spent time in the military or in Vietnam.

On the last page of the dossier, there was a phone number listed as Abraham's last known. I picked up the phone and dialed the number. I didn't recognize the area code.

A recording came on at the other end: *"You reaching Mrs. Kim Video Emporium. Located intersection San Tomas and San Carlos. Open twenty-four hour every day. Like Nited State post office."*

The street names sounded familiar, but I didn't know where they were. One thing was clear: I had a lead. Hopefully, it would take me to Abraham.

CHAPTER 32
Mrs. Kim's Video Emporium

Mrs. Kim's Video Emporium was a small concrete box in a desolate banlieue some six hours north of L.A. According to the colorful brochure I picked up at the tourist bureau, the town had originally been settled by prune farmers from southern Europe. It was now a miniature Chinatown, populated by Vietnamese, Cambodians, and pinoys.

All along the street, there were signs written in indecipherable Asian symbols, and the air reeked of alcohol and rotting cabbage.

I parked my German sedan in the parking lot and stepped inside. A door chime sounded, and a middle-aged Asian woman with gray hair pulled back tightly in a bun shouted from behind the counter, "New release in back!"

When I just stood there without saying anything, she looked up at me and said, "I say we have new release in back."

"Is there a manager I can speak to?" I asked.

She turned stiff and wary. "What this about?"

"I'm looking for a man named Abraham Tomic. He's listed your store as his address. He's come into some money, and I'd really like to find him."

She picked up a phone from under the counter and whispered something into it. Just behind her, there was a large poster for *American Drifter* with a smiling Rex holding a gun to his temple.

The woman put the phone down and said, "The manager will see you now."

She stepped out from behind the counter and began walking toward the back. Her stomach protruded like Rosalyn's. Despite this impediment, which forced her to lean her torso back, she moved quickly past the labyrinth of shelves and videos.

I followed her through a door in the back marked "Employees Only." It opened to a small room the size of a Bogota bathroom. Against the wall, two dozen VCRs were stacked on top of one another. The other walls were filled with glossy video sleeves featuring women with breasts the size of volleyballs.

"There's no one here," I said.

The woman pulled out a gun from her pocket and pointed it at me. "Up against the wall, motherfucker."

I did as she instructed and pressed my hands against the wall. She frisked me carefully, running her hands up and down my back and each of my legs, then shoved the barrel of the gun hard into the back of my head.

"Who are you and what the hell do you want?" she said. Her accent was gone, and she spoke perfect English.

"My name's Boy Genius, and I told you before. I'm looking for a man named Abraham Tomic."

"Bullshit."

"I'm not lying, Ma'am. I've got some money for Abraham. I'd like to make sure he gets it."

"How d'you know Abraham?"

"Abraham and I are old friends. He did me a favor once. I'd like to pay him back."

"You're full of shit. Abraham ain't friends with no whiteboys. He made me promise him that I'd shoot any whiteboy who came around asking for him!"

"I'm not a whiteboy."

"I may be old and pregnant, but I certainly ain't blind."

"I swear to you. This is all a big misunderstanding."

"Yeah, right."

I had only one chance to prove to her that I wasn't a cracker. In my loudest, clearest Korean, I shouted, "Admiral Yi Sun-Shin was one of the greatest military leaders and patriots Korea has ever produced! Born to a humble yet patriotic family from Cholla

Province, he lived from 1545 to 1598 and beat back two Japanese naval invasions, first in 1592 then in 1597. Both were led by Toyotomi Hideyoshi, the monkey-faced emperor who united Japan. Yi Sun-Shin saved Korea with a fleet of Turtle Ships, fire-breathing iron-clad warships that looked like their namesake. After he drove off the first invasion, he was dismissed from office by his enemies through political intrigue. He was called back to his post only after Korea suffered major naval defeats during the second invasion and was on the brink of utter devastation. With just twelve ships, Yi Sun-Shin drove away the Japanese and saved the country, only to have his heroic career ended by a chance enemy bullet from the retreating Japanese. Long live the Republic! Long live His Excellency the Honorable President Park!"

The woman put her gun down and clapped wildly. "Well done. Bravo!"

I turned around slowly and faced her. "I may look like this on the outside, Ma'am. But I'm no whiteboy."

She nodded sympathetically, then sat down on a cardboard box and held up a pack of cigarettes. I took one, and she lit my cigarette and hers.

For a moment, I thought I had been transported back to the storage room where Choco Joe and I'd had so much fun a lifetime earlier.

She took a long drag and said, "His Excellency was a great man. Not like the others. He really cared about the people. Do you know he never wore a Rolex? Never. People saved their money to send him Rolexes by the hundreds, but he never wore them. He was too humble. Even when he died, he had on a cheap Timex. That's the kind of man he was. Anyway, I'm sorry I almost killed you. No hard feelings. It's just with you looking the way you do, I had no choice."

"Do you know where I can find Abraham?"

She blew a thick cloud of smoke and flicked her ash on the carpeted floor. "He used to work for me for a little bit. I had him vacuum the floor and clean the basement. I liked him. Not a smart man, but honest and funny. I could always use some laughter in my life. I may not look it, but I've been through a lot. I lost my entire family on that plane that went down in Russia. My husband and my son. It's a terrible thing to lose your family, a terrible, terrible thing."

I nodded sympathetically.

She sighed and continued, "Some people think the plane didn't go down. There are lots of theories. Some of it's just bunk, what psychologists would call wishful thinking. But there are others that are not so easy to dismiss. For example, there are people who claim that the North Koreans captured the plane. Other people say the Japanese or the Americans shot it down deliberately to make the Russians look bad."

"Do you know where Abraham is?"

"I wanted him to stay here with me, but he didn't want to settle down. He told me it was because he was no good. I got the sense he was running away from something. He'd never tell me though. You know how some men can be. He kept a lot to himself. I'm sure of that. Are you really a friend of Abe's?"

I nodded. "He gave me some very good advice once. I took it and it saved my life. I owe him."

"That why you look the way you do now?"

"It's got a little to do with it."

"I hope you're telling me the truth. The only people who ever came by asking for him were bill collectors and men from the government. Ain't none of them was any good."

"I'm not trying to get money from him. I swear to you."

"You sure?"

I nodded.

"I don't know why, but I trust you. Your Korean has the same accent as His Excellency's. That tells me your heart's in the right place." She jotted something on a piece of paper and handed it to me. "You'll find him there."

I studied the address. It was back in Los Angeles.

"Thank you," I said.

"Don't mention it." She then clicked her heels together and saluted me.

I clicked my heels together and saluted her back. From inside her stomach, I heard a third salute.

CHAPTER 33
Ukulele

The address led to a rundown shop in the middle of a ghetto block that appeared to have been ravaged by twenty years of civil war between people who worshipped different statues. Nearly every door on the block was boarded up, and large chunks of concrete were missing from the walls and the sidewalk where I could only imagine bullets had hit.

The crudely painted sign above the plate glass window said, *"Zeke's Flowers."*

I parked in front and got out of the car just as a young black boy who looked to be about twelve walked up to me and said, "Mister, I'll guard your car for five dollars." His teeth and skin were even whiter and blacker, respectively, than Choco Joe's.

I pretended that the boy was a ghost and started to walk past him, but he quickly motioned with his chin to the corner. There, a dozen young black men were standing shirtless. Their pants were loose and hung low on their hips, and colorful bandanas and baseball caps rested precariously on the edge of their heads. Their wiry bodies were lean and muscular, and it didn't take much effort for me to picture their ancestors crouched low against the earth picking cotton. One young man locked eyes with me and told me without ever uttering a sound that he wished I were dead. I tried to turn him and his friends into ghosts, but my knees started to shake.

The young boy at my side tugged at my sleeve. "There's no telling what crazy niggers out here will do to a nice car like this, mister. They got a ton of bricks and bottles. But if you want, mister, I'll stand here and make sure no one messes with your car.

Make sure no one scratches it up or tries to break inside. How's that sound, mister?"

Five American dollars was enough money to buy a hacienda in the Philippines or a palace in Pakistan. Still, it was a small price to pay to keep a platoon of angry young black men away from my private property. I reached into my pocket, took out my wallet, and handed him a five-dollar bill.

"Make sure no one messes with the car and there will be another five dollars when I come back."

He nodded and promptly put the money away.

I couldn't help marveling at the boy's street smarts and business savvy. In a few years, he would undoubtedly find gainful employment at a fast-food restaurant. In ten years, he would work his way up to night-shift supervisor. Someday, he might even become a proud franchise owner.

The front door of the store was unlocked, and I stepped inside. A soft metal chime sounded, but no one came to greet me. I took the opportunity to look around the place. It wasn't much of a store. The only thing that could be construed as inventory were a half dozen dried-up dandelions kept in a beat-up aluminum pail and a claw-foot bathtub filled with potting soil with nothing growing out of it. Just behind that there was a cheap plastic display case. Inside, there was a silver ukulele. It was dusty and beat-up, but there was no doubt that it looked very much like the one that Abraham had strummed back in Bogota.

As I stared at this artifact from my past, the sound of a toilet flushing echoed through the store. A small door in the back creaked open and a tall old black man popped outside.

The second he spotted me, the old man muttered, "Get out of here."

His hair was gray and cropped close to his head, and his face was clean-shaven with no razor bumps or blemishes.

I pointed to the instrument and said, "Sir, could you tell me whose ukulele that is?"

He shook his head angrily. "That ain't for sale."

"I'd just like to know who it belongs to."

"What fo?" he said, looking me up and down suspiciously.

"It's a fine instrument."

"Sure, it's a fine instrument. That why you think it's suspicious that a black man has it?"

"I didn't mean any disrespect, sir. I'd just like to talk to the person it belongs to."

"I said it before and I'll say it again: What fo?"

"I'd just like to hear how it sounds."

"Five dollars."

"What?"

"Five dollars, and you'll hear how sweet she sounds." He held out his palm. His fingers were long and thin like wooden chopsticks.

I took a five-dollar bill from my wallet and handed it to him. The familiar Lincoln face disappeared quickly into the old man's pocket.

Then, the old man took the ukulele out from the display case, wiped the dust off with his hands, and began strumming. His long bony fingers danced expertly across the strings. He nodded in time to the music and screeched, at the top of his lungs, *"Kung fu comes from China! Do monks eat Aunt Ja-mima? Karate or kung fuey! Both can kill yo daddy!"*

The familiar lyrics punched me in the face.

When he finished playing, the old man grinned and said, "I'll play another song for ten bucks."

"Where'd you learn that song?" I asked.

"I ain't learnt nothing. How's a man gonna learn something that he done created from thin air?"

"You made up that song?"

"Ain't that what I just said? What's wrong with you? Can't believe that a black man is capable of writing songs?"

"Sir, it's really important that I talk with the person who wrote that song. I'm an old friend of his."

"Are you deaf or just plain stupid? What did I just say? I done told you I wrote that damn song, didn't I? Now show me some money or get the hell out of here. I ain't got no time for pussy-footing. You wanna hear another song, pay me ten dollars. Otherwise, get the hell out of my store."

I looked hard into his eyes. He was clearly a black man, yet he'd just sang the same song that Abraham had sung in Bogota.

I took out ten dollars and handed it to him.

He snatched it from me and again strummed his ukulele. *"This world sucks. The good die. The bad die. Everybody dies. All together now. This world sucks. The young die. The old die. Everybody dies."*

It was the same song that Abraham had sung at my parents' funeral. That had been the last I'd ever seen him. "Sir, do you know where I can find Abraham Tomic?"

The old man's eyes lit up for a second. "Who you say you was looking fo?"

"A man named Abraham Tomic."

"Who dat?"

"He's an old friend of mine. He did me a favor once. I'd like to pay him back."

"Never heard of him."

"Sir, I'm not a bill collector and I'm not from the government. I'm just an old friend and I would really like to talk with him."

"I don't care who you are, son. You could be the governor of Illinois for all I care, I ain't never heard of no Abraham Shabraham. Whoever you're looking for, you're barking up the wrong flower. If you ain't figured it out by now, this here is the ghetto. Folks look like you ain't supposed to come around this way unless they're crazy or lost."

"Sir, please. It's really important that I see him. Please."

"I told you already. I ain't never heard of the man. Now get out of my store and go on back to wherever you from. This may be the ghetto, but I got friends in the police. All I gots to do is pick up the phone and the police will be here in minutes to cart your sorry ass away."

"I'm not trying to hurt the guy, sir. I've come into some money recently, and I'd like to make sure he gets his fair share."

"You say money is involved?"

"Yes, sir."

"How much money you talkin' about?"

"Not a lot. After taxes and expenses, it comes to just about $4,000," I lied.

"Four thousand, you say?"

"Yes, sir. And, of course, I'd be more than happy to pay you a finder's fee. How does $400 sound?"

"That sounds like just ten percent. I'd need more than that. But let's not get ahead of ourselves. What'd you say your name was again?"

"My name's Boy Genius."

His face turned dark and angry. "Get the hell out of my store! If I ever see your sorry white ass in here again, I'll kill you. You hear me?" He pushed me toward the door and held up his ukulele as if to swing it at me.

I didn't know what had brought about his sudden change, but I realized there was no point in trying to reason with the man any longer. The ukulele appeared to be Abraham's, and the songs the old man sang were definitely the same ones Abraham had sung. But it was clear that the old man wasn't going to fill me in on any details.

I started for the door, but before I could reach it, a brick flew in through the plate-glass window, splattering a hundred shards onto the floor. Immediately, the old man rushed over and picked up the brick. "Motherfuckers," he muttered, shaking his head.

He hurried behind the cash register and took out a shotgun from underneath the counter. Waving the heavy weapon, he stormed past me and rushed out the door.

I followed him to the door and peered outside. My car was gone, and the enterprising boy whom I had entrusted to guard the car was nowhere in sight. I had little doubt that my car would eventually make its way to a black market in Nigeria. I

171

just hoped my insurance policy covered irrevocable losses to the ghetto.

On the opposite side of the street, a dozen black men were crouched behind an abandoned sofa. The tops of their prominent Afros shook from time to time above the edge of the sofa. Without a word, the old man pointed his shotgun toward them and fired two shots. Each shot sounded like a cannon exploding.

"None of you lazy bastards are gonna get my store. You hear me?" he shouted. "I ain't come out here to this godforsaken city just to hand over my wealth to some poor niggers who should know better."

Bricks and bottles flew from across the street and landed in front of the store. More bricks and bottles followed, forcing the old man to retreat inside.

The old man bolted the door shut behind him. "Motherfuckers got another thing coming if they think they can take my store away from me. I'm gonna fight to keep what's mine. As the saying goes, the brick stops here."

He rushed around behind the counter again and started loading large brass bullets into his shotgun. More bricks rained in through the broken window.

"What's going on, sir?" I said.

"You just mind your own damn business. This ain't got a motherfucking thing to do with you."

A heavy bottle burst through the window, crashed on the floor, and burst into flame. The old man tried to stomp the fire out, but it was futile. More bottles flew in. The flames spread, and soon the store was filled with smoke.

I grabbed the old man by the arms and shook him. "How do I get out of here?"

He motioned with his chin to the front door. "There ain't no way to get out except through there. But the moment you set your foot out that way, twelve angry niggers will jump your ass and beat you till all your organs are crushed and you die from internal bleeding. They'll do it even though they ain't never seen your ass around here before 'cuz they angry and crazy and they gots nothing to lose."

"You don't have a back door?"

He shook his head. "There was one a long time ago, but I had to seal it shut 'cuz punks was breaking in and stealing my flowers."

"There's no other way out?"

"Not unless you can flush yourself down the toilet into the sewers."

I felt the blood rush out of me. After all I had lived through, I would now die in a run-down flower shop in a godforsaken North American ghetto.

I sat down on the floor with my back against the counter wall. Flames danced in front of me and smoke gathered up above me like a thick winter comforter.

The old man fired his shotgun in the direction of the street, then turned to me. "How much money you wanna offer me for the ukulele?"

I had to hand it to the man: He was a businessman. I took out all the cash from my wallet. It came to a little more than a hundred dollars. He said, "It's not much, but I'll take it. She's all yours." He shoved the money into his pocket, then handed me the ukulele.

I ran my fingers along the fingerboard and touched the strings. There was no mistaking it. It was the very same instrument that Abraham had used to entertain me when I was a boy.

Angry that I would die without getting revenge, I grabbed its neck, raised it high above me, and swung it down like an axe against the floor. It cracked in half. From inside its body, out popped a dozen Bazooka Joe's and a large firecracker the size of a magic marker.

The old smiled and said, "What d'you know? I'd forgot all about that."

I picked up the firecracker and said, "What good is this?"

"It's T-N-T good. That stands for Takes No Time to blow a motherfucking hole through this wall."

He snatched the dynamite from me and hurried to the back wall. There, he bent down low, set the stick on the ground, and lit the fuse. I crouched for cover under the counter.

Exactly 2.65 seconds later, a loud bang thundered through the air and the earth shook. When I looked back up, there was a small hole at the base of the wall.

"What you waitin' fo, son?" the old man said, grinning widely and pointing at the hole that looked like it was just big enough for a dog to crawl through.

I dropped to the floor and started snaking through. My head squeezed through, then one shoulder and the next.

"Go on now. You're almost there," the old man shouted from behind me.

My arms got through, then my chest. But then, there was resistance.

"What's the matter? Why'd you stop all of a sudden?"

"I'm stuck!"

The old man pushed me from behind, and a jolt of pain shot up from Jesus, forcing me to scream. Amidst the fire and the excitement, too much blood had been pumped into Jesus, and he was wedged tightly against the wall.

"What's wrong, son?"

"I'm stuck."

"I know you're stuck. Just suck your stomach in."

"It's not my stomach."

The old man was silent for a second, then shouted, "Goddamn, son! The building's about to go down in flames, you got twelve angry niggers running at your heels and a crazy old black man with a shotgun standing behind you, how you gonna go and get yourself an erection at a time like this? You cracker sons-of-bitches and yo' dicks. Everything but yo' dick's done made it to the promised land."

It was true. I had to calm Jesus down as quickly as I could or else I would burn to a crisp. I thought of Ms. Sommers's leathery old face. I thought of Tanh and a boatful of grimy little refugees fighting for food scraps. I thought of Dr. Namumanu's metal hooks. I thought of Mother and Father and the peasants picking their noses in the rice paddies of Father's village. But nothing seemed to be able to calm Jesus down. I could do nothing except wait.

Meanwhile, I peered up and took a good long look at freedom. It was a run-down school bus sitting on cinder blocks in the middle of an abandoned lot filled with broken bottles. Smoke filtered from an iron pipe sticking out of the window, and the sounds of Spanish television floated out. A piece of rope hung between the bus and a tall two-by-four stuck in the ground. On the rope, dirty laundry of various sizes fluttered against the sky. Directly below a white undershirt, a goat with bulging eyes was snacking on a red Coca-Cola can while a fat chicken clucked noisily next to it.

The idea that whoever was living in the bus, most likely a family of Puerto Ricans, was doing so rent-free with fresh goat milk and eggs to boot, zapped all chi out of Jesus and I finally managed to slip through to freedom. Exactly at that moment, from inside the bus, a Spanish broadcaster shouted, *"Goooooooooooooal!"*

I got up on my feet and patted the dirt off myself. Then, I crouched down low and looked back into the hole. The old man peered up at me from inside and smiled. His teeth were perfectly straight.

I stretched a hand out toward him and said, "Come on. Give me your hand."

The old man shrank back slightly, then shook his head. "I ain't going." There was a strange smile on his face.

"Your store's burning down. You can't stay in there."

"I ain't going. I ain't got no place to go to. This here is the only home I got left. A man ain't nothing without a home. I learned that from my mama."

"But you'll die if you stay inside."

"It don't make much of a difference. I'm an old man. I ain't got no more than a few years left anyhow. Except for this store, I ain't got a damn motherfucking thing. I'm too old to live on my wits or hard labor. I know for a fact that it's all downhill from here."

"Please, just come on out. Please."

"I helped you out, so do me just one favor, son. When you get out of here and make it back to safety, tell Boy Genius that Abraham was sorry. Let him know that the man he should be looking for is a tall white man with the letters H-I-J scarred on his cheek."

"A tall white man?"

He nodded, then moved away from the hole and disappeared from view. A moment later, there were three gunshots. Silence followed, and then the crackling sound of fire eating its way up the walls.

I turned around and began walking as far away from the fire as possible. Neither the goat nor the chicken said anything. From inside the bus, a woman screamed out as if she were being stabbed. Then there was silence and a loud cry. Through the windows, I could see an old pair of hands holding up a newborn infant. Not a second after one poor bastard had died, here was another to take his place.

I crossed the empty lot and made my way through an alley that ran behind a row of dilapidated houses.

Earlier that morning, I had hoped to gain inner peace. I had nothing of the kind. Instead, I felt even more restless than before.

Up ahead, an eerie glow was coming from a convenience store. I moved closer, hoping someone there would be able to help me.

A mob of brown people carrying torches was standing outside the store, murmuring secret messages to one another in Hmong, Mexican, and Ebonics. The fire, burning angrily from their torches, cast creepy shadows on their faces.

From inside the store, a middle-aged Asian man wearing a cheap polyester shirt with the sleeves rolled up to his elbows waved a broom at the crowd and shouted, "Go different store! Go different store!"

His English had the same North Kyoungsang accent that

Father and His Excellency had had, and I knew that he was a compatriot.

I strode through the crowd, making a point to swing my arms forcefully at my side. Like all good people of color, they were startled to see a tall white man in a suit and promptly moved aside to form a clear path for me.

Behind the broom-waving store owner, colorful fruits and vegetables were stacked neatly on cardboard boxes that were sitting on top of plastic milk crates. The way the nectarines had been placed neatly next to the peaches confirmed that the broom-waving gentleman had indeed been born in the Hermit Kingdom. He rushed up to me and said, "Help me, sir. Please help me."

He looked more afraid than any man should. I'm not sure if it was his North Kyoungsang accent or the desperate look in his eyes, but something prompted me to take action. I turned to the mob of ex-cons and incorrigibly poor people. Their faces were hard and expressionless and their eyes were red. The mob eyed me nervously, as if waiting for me to speak. From the back, someone shouted, "Move out of the way, gringo!"

The store owner waved his broom again and yelled, "Go different store! Go different store!" He sounded more helpless than ever.

The mob took a step forward. Only three feet separated them from me. The store owner glanced at me. "They should go different store. Why they no go different store?"

I had to act. I reached behind me and picked up a nectarine from the display. Fortunately, it wasn't yet ripe. I hurled the fruit as hard as I could through the store window. The glass shattered magnificently into a hundred sharp shards. Immediately, the crowd rushed forward and pushed past us into the store. Within seconds, people were overturning shelves and carrying boxes of groceries and fruit out of the store.

A Mexican woman wearing a red Marlboro cap stormed out of the store balancing two cases of Budweiser on her head. It was the same method for carrying heavy loads that Mother had used. As I marveled at the woman's skill and balance, more and more people crept out of doorways and joined the growing mob. Some people overturned parked cars. Others threw bricks and set fire to awnings. Soon, the entire block was on fire.

After the mob swarmed away to the next block, the store owner turned to me and said indignantly, "Why you throw nectarine? Why you throw nectarine?"

I said nothing. My heart went out to him, but there was no way I could explain to him that I had most probably saved his life.

Angry but unable to work up the courage to attack a white man, he crouched down on the sidewalk and stared blankly at the fire dancing in front of him. His livelihood was going up in flames and so were the cushy careers he'd envisioned for his children. I could picture him later at home, telling his children that they would have to live the same hard life that he'd had to live because a white man had refused to help him fend off an angry mob of communists.

Scattered among the madness and the fires that were sprouting up all around us, a hundred bow-legged peasants cried hysterically and screamed obscenities at the sky in the language I'd first heard inside Mother's womb. They all looked exactly like Mother and Father. As I strolled past them, it dawned on me that even though these shopkeepers had fled 12,000 miles around the world, they had been born refugees, and a refugee destiny was catching up with them.

When I rounded the corner, a shirtless young black man stepped up in front of me and blocked my path. He looked to be about nineteen and had a blue bandanna wrapped around his head. His wiry but muscular torso was covered with a dozen tattoos. Most of them were Chinese pictograms. Exactly in the middle of his chest where a butterfly might have been, there was the same pictogram for "will" that had hung in His Excellency's study.

The black man glowered at me and said, "What the fuck you doing here, you cracker son-of-a-bitch?"

I looked up at him. "I'm just passing through, son. I've got nothing to do with anything here."

That didn't seem to appease him. He leaned his face close to mine. "First of all, I ain't your son. And it's crackers like you that started all this shit in the first place. It's crackers like you that's what's wrong with the world."

His breath reeked of cheap beer and barbecue sauce. "Listen, you got this all wrong. I have nothing to do with what happened here today. I don't even live here."

He frowned and shook his head. "I know you don't live here, motherfucker. You came down here looking to score or you took a wrong turn off the freeway. I know that."

A crowd of angry onlookers was gathering around us. All were waiting eagerly for the black man to kill me. I reached into my pocket and took out my wallet. All my cash was gone. I had given it to the old man back at the flower shop. I took out my credit cards and my ATM card and waved them in front of me. "I'm out of cash, but if you direct me to an ATM machine, I'd be more than happy to withdraw as much money as I can for you."

He knocked the cards out of my hand. "That's what's wrong with all you crackers. Y'all think we're out to rob you. What the fuck is that about, man? You don't even know me. You don't even fucking know me! What makes you think you can offer me money and make everything all right? Did I even ask for your money? Did I, motherfucker?"

I took a deep breath and looked up at the sky. When my black friend followed my gaze, I began running back down the street. The black man and the throng of onlookers chased after me. As I ran past the Korean store owner whose life I'd saved earlier, he shouted, "Kill him! Kill cracker!"

Though I knew it was futile to try to outspeed a ruthless gang of angry young black males whose ancestors had run to catch antelopes and cheetahs in the altitude of the African plains, I pumped my arms and ran as never before in my life. Even Mr. Sohn, the marathon king, would have been proud of me.

I turned the corner. Up ahead, there was a tractor-trailer stopped in the middle of the street. A white driver stared at me from inside the cab.

I waved my arms maniacally and sped toward him. I didn't care whether he was crazy or lost; I was just happy that I wasn't the only white man in the 'hood.

Just then, a popping sound pierced the air. As I took my next step, a throbbing sensation gripped the entire left side of my body, and I fell to the ground. My chin bounced against the pavement, and I heard the crunch of breaking bone.

Flat on my stomach, I peered up at the roof of a one-story building across the street. Crouched there on one knee was a man in riot gear holding a semi-automatic rifle.

He stood up slowly and took off his gas mask. There was no mistaking the face or the large aviator sunglasses. It was His Excellency the Most Honorable President Park. Not a hair was out of place, and the bastard looked better than ever.

My body felt as if it were on fire. Still, I mustered all my strength to give Him the finger. He just smiled.

That was the last thing I saw before I blacked out and died. And so, just as Mother's wizened old father had prophesied in an airport on the other side of the world, I became the third and final member of my clan to perish in the harsh soil of North America.

BOOK IV

The Book of the Dead

BOOK IV

CHAPTER 34
The End of the Tunnel

All was dark except for a speck of white light in the far distance. Just to my right, the giant head of General Douglas MacArthur hovered, complete with his Aviator sunglasses and signature pipe.

As I walked toward the speck of light, the giant head followed me and hollered, "You've got a mighty fine spleen, soldier! Use the spleen to go to the light!"

"But I'm tired, General!" I shouted.

"Don't be silly, soldier. No true soldier's ever tired. 'Cuz in war there's no substitute for victory. Old soldiers never die. They just fade away."

A cold clammy hand shook my shoulder and a different voice called out to me, "Forget old soldiers and wake the hell up!"

I opened my eyes. Slowly, a dark dungeon-like basement came into view. Three feet in front of me, a large hunched figure was staring intently at me.

"Where am I?" I asked.

The figure just cackled.

"Where am I?" I repeated.

"This is heaven on earth and you're the guest of honor. Like the prophet from Bethlehem, Lazarus, and Osiris, you were once dead, but now you are alive. Hallelujah!"

"Who are you?"

"That's not important. A better question is, were there ever tigers in Africa?"

"What?"

"According to fossil evidence, tigers don't appear to have ever existed in Africa, yet there's a word for tiger in many tribal languages and the tiger plays a significant role in much tribal folklore. This leads to the obvious hypothesis that tigers may have roamed that continent at some point in the past. Of course, this then leads to the corollary question of what happened to wipe them out."

"Is there a light we can turn on?"

"Okay, but you asked for it."

He clapped twice and a small naked bulb lit up above us.

When the figure in front of me came into clearer view, I immediately regretted my hasty request for illumination. Crouched before me was the largest Oriental man I'd ever seen. He was rounder and bigger than the most fervent practitioners of sumo. But his sheer volume wasn't his most prominent feature. It was his face. It had been grotesquely scarred, and the skin on the left side of his face was sinewy and fibrous. I knew it wasn't polite to stare at such a deformity, but I simply couldn't help myself.

The man smiled sheepishly, then said, "I was burned as a boy. Looks pretty gruesome, doesn't it?"

"I'm sorry."

"Don't be. What happened wasn't your fault. It had nothing to do with you."

I nodded politely, then started to get up. Immediately, a piercing pain shot up through my left leg and pulled me back to the ground. I cringed and moaned. It felt as if a ten-penny nail were being pounded straight into my kneecap.

"Easy there. You've been hurt pretty badly. A bullet pierced your left lung, and your leg's been shot up a half dozen times. I took the bullets out, but you won't be walking for quite a while. If you ask me, it's a miracle you're alive again."

The pain in my leg grew intense, and I let out a feral cry.

The stranger covered his ears, then handed me a small blue pill. "Here, take this."

The pill was the size of a dime, had no writing on it, and didn't look like it came from a pharmacy. Still, I wasn't in any position to be picky. Like a drowning man who grabs at whatever is thrown before him, the intensifying pain shooting up my leg forced me to take the pill. The pain quickly went away and a pleasant numbness came over my entire body.

My strange host smiled. "Feels like you're floating on a cloud, doesn't it?"

I nodded. It really did feel like that, and I couldn't help smiling. "What was that I just took?"

He grinned like a Cheshire cat. "It's called Indira."

"Indira?"

"It shoots a thousand volts of pure adrenaline smack into the left and right ventricles of your heart and gets the blood pumping again. I developed it myself. You see, unlike some other sciences, chemistry has many practical applications. That's why more than twenty-five multinational pharmaceutical giants have been plotting to steal Indira from me for the last twelve years. They want to mass produce it and unleash it in the ghetto. But I won't let them."

"Where am I?"

He cupped one hand over his right ear and then put the index finger of his other hand in front of his mouth. "Hear that?"

There was a soft humming sound coming through the ceiling.

The stranger smiled and said, "It's a carefully orchestrated symphony, only without instruments or musicians. That's the beauty of it, you see. It's music in its purest form."

"Where's the humming coming from?"

"You tell me, my friend."

"I don't know. It sounds like machines of some sort."

He clapped his hands together. "You are clever, aren't you! It *is* from machines. It's the sound of clothes tumbling round and round inside a hot metal drum. There are fifty dryers and forty washing machines in my laundromat, and not one is ever out of order. I make sure of that. That's why I've succeeded where others have failed. Anyway, you needn't worry about a thing. The police will never find you here."

"What are you talking about?"

"You don't remember, do you?" He peered intently at me, then answered his own question. "You're a wanted man. The police are out looking for you. You killed a man during the riots."

"I didn't kill anyone."

"But you did. A young black man. I saw you. You leapt on him and smashed his head open with a beer bottle. You were screaming, 'Nigger! Nigger! Nigger!'"

I had no recollection whatsoever of the scene he was describing.

He smiled and continued, "It's a good thing I happened by when I did. Had the mob caught up to you, they would have torn you to pieces with their bare hands. Anyway, you don't want to be out there now. The rioting's turned quite ugly. Chicago, Washington, D.C., New York. The entire country's engulfed by it. Some people are calling it a full-blown civil war. Everywhere blacks are killing whites. Whites are killing blacks. Mexicans are siding with blacks in most cities, and with whites in the suburbs. And as for Asians, people who look like me, we're being hunted down by both sides. It seems neither side can trust us completely." He cackled as though he found the horrific scenario he described to be unbearably funny.

I didn't know whether to believe him. The riot I had seen had looked like the start of an outright revolt, but I had no way of knowing what was really going on in the outside world.

The pain returned to my leg, even stronger than before. I winced and let out a horrific scream.

My host smiled and said, "One thing I forgot to tell you about my Indira: She's wonderful, but their effect, I'm afraid, is only temporary." He then took out another pill from his pocket. "Tell you what I'll do, I'll give you as many pills as you need, but you have to promise me you'll lie down and rest. Is it a deal?"

I nodded begrudgingly, then quickly swallowed the pill my host gave me. Once again, it took effect immediately, and the pain ebbed away as if it'd never been there.

My host smiled and said, "Truth is, I've been hoping for something like this to happen. I never thought it would, but it did.

You just don't know how happy all this makes me. You just don't know, Boy Genius."

His uttering my name startled me. I scanned his face. "Who the hell are you? And how the hell do you know my name?"

He clapped his hands together in front of his chest and convulsed with pleasure. "It is you! I knew it. I just knew it! They said you looked different now and you do, but I knew it was you. There's only one person in the world who would get hunted down like that. I bet you never thought we'd meet like this. It's a strange world, isn't it? The world's nothing but one t-t-tiny ins-s-sane as-s-sylum. Now l-l-look at me. I'm so damn excit-t-ted I'm s-t-t-tu-t-tering. It's the ugliest thing in the world, stuttering is. I would give just about anything not to stutter. But you wouldn't understand, would you? I'll bet you've never stuttered in your whole life."

It was then that the identity of my disfigured Oriental host came to me. His stuttering was a big clue, but it was the shape of his face more than anything else that revealed his identity. Even though it had been disfigured in a gruesome manner, his face was still a perfect circle.

"Lucky Chang?" I said.

He smiled sheepishly and scratched the back of his head. "Bingo! It took you a while, but you hit the nail on the donkey. I wish I could give you a trip for two to Ochos Cascadas, but I don't think you're ready for such an excursion. At least not yet."

"What are you doing here?"

He cackled again inexplicably. "I wish I could tell you, Boy Genius. I wish I knew. L-l-long l-l-live the Republic. L-l-l-long l-live H-H-His Excellency the Most Honorable President Park. What a joke. What a magnificent sham. Did you know that I never wanted to be on TV? All I ever wanted was to stay with my father in Cheju, to wake up in the morning to the sound of the waves, to smell the salt in the air, and to swim in the sea. I never asked to be a genius. I never asked for any of it. They thought it was one big joke. One big ego trip. 'Look at us. We're so damn powerful that we can take even a country bumpkin and turn him into a genius for the people.' The bastards. Every time I went on the air, I was scared to death that I'd forget to stutter and start talking like myself and those bastards would do with me what they said they'd done to you."

"What are you talking about?"

"They made me stutter, Boy Genius. It was all a lie. Like my red cheeks. They tattooed them that way. I never had red cheeks in my life. And I wasn't a stutterer."

"But you stuttered just a minute ago."

He rolled his eyes and shook his head once. "That only happened after faking it for so long. It's an undesired side effect of years of behavioral conditioning. I stutter now when I get excited. But I swear to you I never stuttered before those bastards put me on TV. But I guess the joke's on them now. I mean, just look at us. Who would have ever imagined we would ever meet like this? I sure didn't. Did you?"

"No, never," I said.

"You know, I used to lay awake at nights when I was a kid wondering what had happened to you. You remember Mr. K, don't you? He used to say, 'Oh, I don't know what happened to the first Boy Genius. They say he's been fed to the lions at the National Zoo, but I think that's just a rumor.' He said it just like that, in that gruff voice of his and that tone of his when you can't tell whether he's kidding or not. It sent a chill down my spine every time. Choco Joe wanted to kill him. He laughed and smiled when the cameras were on, but once they were off, he never said a word to me or anyone else. He hated everyone, especially me. But it wasn't my fault. If it were up to me, I wouldn't have had anything to do with it. I mean it. I hope you don't blame me. Do you, Boy Genius?"

I thought a long while, then said, "I don't." It wasn't exactly the truth, but under the circumstance I didn't think it was wise to antagonize my host.

He breathed a sigh of relief. "You don't know what that means to me, Boy Genius. You don't know what that means."

"How did I get here, Lucky Chang?"

"I dragged you from the rubble before the mob could get to you. Your heart had stopped beating and you were dead. That's when Indira came to the rescue and saved the day. Afterwards, you were unconscious, but I knew it had to be you by the way you kept on babbling about old soldiers."

"What about the part about me killing a man?"

"What about it? Maybe it happened, maybe I made it up. But I can tell you this much. Lots of people died out there, and not all the killers have been caught, including the man who shot you."

"His Excellency shot me."

"You believe what you want, Boy Genius, but I can tell you this: The only truth that matters now is that you're in no shape to walk around. In time, your leg will heal and your mind will clear up. Until then, you've got no choice but to stay here and rest."

"I want to see a doctor," I said.

He beamed. "But you've already seen one. Lucky Chang has M.D.s and Ph.D.s from every school between Seoul and Pusan. You were treated by the most capable surgeon to ever come out of Korea."

"I want to see a less capable doctor."

"I'm afraid that's impossible, Boy Genius. Under the circumstances, you're lucky you're not in some jail cell, fighting for bread crumbs and a corner to pee in."

"But this is all so crazy."

"I can't argue with you there. But now you're starting to make me sad. I thought you'd understand, Boy Genius. Of all the people in the world who should understand, you should. I've been waiting so long to see you. On those nights when I wanted to give up and just end it all, I thought of you and the way you'd fought back, the way you screwed them and told them to go to hell. You were their poster child. You had it all, and you gave it all up so you could live for yourself, as an individual and as a capitalist. Just look at you. You even look like an American, like an American movie star."

Suddenly, I was overcome by a great sense of shame. I lowered my eyes and stared at the floor.

"I wish everyone back home could see you now, Boy Genius. They'd get a kick out of your new look. You really made it."

"Look, Lucky Chang, about my decision to leave . . ."

"It was so brave. You told them to screw themselves even though you knew full well that such a decision could be dangerous."

"It wasn't like that. I had no choice. There was nothing heroic about it!"

He frowned. "But that's not true. You're being overly modest. I know for a fact that you could have stayed on and eked out a living as a cram-school instructor. That would have shown tacit support for the regime, but you chose not to do that."

"How do you know all that?" I asked.

"I looked up your files back at KBS," he said matter-of-factly.

"What files?"

"The files in Mr. K's office. Anyway, what I want to know is how does it feel? How does it feel to know that you and I have outlived Punk Leader Park and his cronies?"

"What did you call Him?"

"Punk Leader Park," he repeated. "It's no big deal, Boy Genius. We can call him whatever we want. He's dead and gone." He paused and peered at me intently. "You do know he's dead, right?"

I nodded.

"You're not still stuck calling him by that ridiculous title of his, are you?"

I couldn't answer him. I suddenly felt like the biggest coward.

"My goodness, Boy Genius. What happened to you? You were our hero. We looked up to you. If anyone would be free from that punk's grip, we thought it'd be you."

I sat up. "Well, you thought wrong."

"I can see that."

I didn't like the tone of his voice. It was too accusatory, and there was also a trace of scorn. Neither of us said anything for a while.

"I guess we were wrong about you," he said, finally breaking the silence.

"Who's this *we* you keep referring to?" I said.

"All the geniuses that Punk Leader Park pimped, of course."

"What geniuses?"

"There were tons of us. Thousands. Some excelled in music, others in math. Still others were sent as infants by the KCIA to families around the world. It was a systemic and methodical way to destabilize foreign governments and speed up the intelligence-gathering process. All of us, all the children whose lives were forever changed by the regime, looked up to you, Boy Genius. I couldn't have lived through the changes otherwise."

"What changes?"

He stood up and started pacing the small room. He had a slight limp and seemed to favor his right leg. "The ones that came with that bastard Chun. It was wretched. As cruel and deluded as Park was, there was a noble side to him. He was almost aristocratic. In comparison, Chun was so utterly despicable and lacking in anything even remotely redeeming. The first thing he did when he came to power was to lift the midnight curfew. Innkeepers throughout the country protested, fearing they'd lose business. On the contrary, their businesses thrived. People went to motels not to sleep through the curfew but to screw like rabbits. He turned the entire country into a brothel."

"How did you end up here?" I asked.

"I got out as soon as I could. They wouldn't let me, but I found my own way out. It wasn't easy, but I don't regret it for a second." He pointed to his face. "A little benzene and a match is all it took. It wasn't even very painful. When it was over, I wondered why I hadn't done it sooner. They told the public it was a car accident. The important thing, was they couldn't put me on the air, not without scaring the children. I shipped out soon after the Olympics. I've been running this laundromat ever since. Back there, I was a television star, but here I'm just another groveling immigrant making a living cleaning other people's underwear."

He smiled, somewhat bitterly. "Anyway, you need to rest. We can talk more later."

He handed me a tall vial of pills, then turned around and left the room through a heavy metal door. The door slammed shut behind him, then I heard the lock click. The pain returned to my leg. Quickly, I downed another pill and let Indira wipe my troubles away.

CHAPTER 35
Checkpoint Charlie

Aside from the fact that Lucky Chang wouldn't let me out of the basement, he was a most perfect host. He cared for me diligently. He cleaned my wound and supplied me with all the painkillers I needed. And three times a day, he brought me fresh tacos.

Within a week, my leg grew stronger and I could walk again. But I couldn't get myself to leave the basement. Unwittingly, I had grown addicted to Indira and depended on Lucky Chang to supply me with more pills. I tried to cut myself off from this fiendish dependency, but the euphoria brought on by Indira was too great. It helped me forget about all those who had turned my life into a battlefield.

Soon, Lucky Chang stopped bothering even to lock the door to my basement room. It was less a signal of trust than a sign of his complete confidence in the power of Indira. But Indira wasn't the panacea I had hoped it would be. As fantastic as it was at erasing whatever was in my mind when I was awake, it was utterly ineffectual in protecting me from the dark thoughts that descended on me as soon as I drifted off to sleep—images of H-I-J butchering Mother and Father as well as pictures of a pregnant Rosalyn reminding me of the 101 ways in which I had failed her. Needless to say, I avoided sleep as much as I could and spent my days in an Indira-induced haze.

But the pills did not come cheap. To get them, I had to indulge Lucky Chang's whim. Night after night, I was forced to watch a musical about General Yi-Sun-Shin on a tiny television and VCR that he wheeled into the basement. It was his favorite film.

THE RETURN OF GENERAL YI-SUN-SHIN

FADE IN.

Yi-Sun-Shin, standing tall—surrounded by a hundred Korean soldiers with strips of white cloth wrapped around their heads—on his magnificent turtle ship. A drummer beats the drums furiously.

He stares out into the sea. In the distance, the Japanese fleet looms ominously, moving ever closer. The Japanese red sun banner, waving in the wind. Taiko drums banging. A battle of drums.

TWO MEN bring A THIRD to General Yi.

MAN #1

General, we have found a stowaway on board.

They push THIRD to his knees, then yank off his headband. Lo and behold, the man is really a WOMAN, with long flowing hair.

YI-SUN-SHIN
(sings)

Dear Soonja, why did you come here?
Didn't I make my wishes clear?
I promised your mother I'd keep you home.
Now I have to make a . . .

WOMAN
(sings)

My mother this, my mother that.
You must really like your women fat.
If you're not glad to see me, just say the word.
I'll go away like bad bean curd.

YI-SUN-SHIN
Why must you always doubt what's in my heart?
I've promised many times we'd never part.

WOMAN
You risk life and limb for battle.
Yet you treat me like mere cattle.

YI-SUN-SHIN
Oh, forgive me, Soonja. Oh, forgive me please.
But I must go and fight the Japanese.
If we don't win today, we'll fight even from the grave.
Or, how else comrades, will we our country ever save?
Hairy enemies from foreign lands creep on our shore.
Long live Korea, the land that we all adore.
Japs and chinks and even bigger monsters from across the seas,
They want our land because ours is the land of the Rhees.

He lifts her up and kisses her passionately. Behind them the
soldiers give the Black Power salute.

FADE TO BLACK.

One night, I ran out of Indira and had no choice but to wander
out of the basement to find Lucky Chang. I reluctantly climbed
up the stairs and went to the ground floor. Heavy metal gates covered the front of the store. Two rows of industrial washing
machines sat empty, staring blankly at me.

I trudged slowly toward the back where there was a door with
a sign that said, "Office." The door was slightly ajar, and as I got
closer, I could hear a loud, rabid, and hysterical voice. I stopped
outside the door and peered inside. The room was filled with
microphones, equalizers, and other broadcasting equipment, and
Lucky Chang was bent over a desk with his back to me. In his left
hand there was a small pistol, and he waved it around wildly as he

spoke into a microphone: "This is El Jefe broadcasting live from the pit of hell. I tell you, it's a beautiful world and it's going to be an even more beautiful place before you know it because the revolution is growing right under your nose and no amount of Disney magic is going to s-s-sweep away the poor and the revolution under its bright lights and sanitized fun. And for us, the ones with guns and nothing to lose, the sweet jihad is within our grasp and all your treasures are nothing but a rusty relic that will be decimated, wiped clean from the face of this democratic earth, a planet whose children were born equal and free before they were enslaved by your paid thugs. But we know different. We're free. Free to live. Free to see. Free to grow up and free to exact justice. It's true what the peasants of old said. Steal a little and they make you a thief. Steal a lot and they make you a king. Those who ride limousines and sip v-v-v-vintage wine. Those who shower the poor with television commercials and billboard ads of the latest technological wonders we can't have. Those who believe money can keep the poor at bay and barbarians at the gate and revolutions in nameless countries f-f-f-far f-f-far away. You ought to be and you will be shot, lined up before a f-f-f-firing squad of bloodthirsty V.C.s who have infiltrated your stronghold as maids and deliverymen. We smile the secret smile of revolution and count the nights till the day of reckoning is at hand. At the dawn of that deadly hour, the T-t-t-twin T-t-t-towers, the Chrysler Building, and the Empire State Building will be no more than shattered tombstones marking the graves of a dead regime. And all the regime's unsuspecting bosses, sirs and madams, who sleep soundlessly on soft waterbeds snuggled underneath duvet comforters, will wake up to a different world, a world turned upside-down and right-side-up in which the ruling class will rule no more and the m-m-masses will be liberated from the chains that enslave them. Up against the wall, m-m-m-motherfucker!"

Lucky Chang then turned his head slowly and stared right at me. There was a strange smile on his face; it occurred to me then that he'd wanted me to come upstairs and hear his tirade. This had been his way of telling me that he was a communist.

We both said nothing for a long while. Then, Lucky Chang took out a vial from a safe on the floor and tossed it toward me. I caught it and trudged back to the basement.

I wasn't sure just what sort of intrigue Lucky Chang was involved with, but I didn't want anything to do with it. I'd been born again, and the only vengeance I sought was on H-I-J.

It was clear I had to leave Lucky Chang, but in order to do so, I first had to free myself from the bondage of pharmaceutical science.

I no longer had the will power that I'd had as a young boy and could not cut myself off completely from a drug as powerful as Indira. Instead, I reduced my dosage. Rather than take twelve pills in a day, I took ten and saved two. Once my body was content with ten pills, I cut down to nine. Gradually, I was able to get by on just two hits of Indira per day.

When I'd saved more than 2,000 pills, enough to last me a thousand days, I made my move. One day, when Lucky Chang brought me a fresh batch of hot tacos, I said, "Listen, Lucky Chang, I think it's time for me to go."

"You're really going to like the tacos today. I made them fresh from s-s-s-scratch."

"Your tacos are always good. But I said it's time I left this place, Lucky Chang."

"But you're not well yet."

"It's nothing personal, Lucky Chang. I'm very grateful that you've helped me all this time. But I can't stay here forever. It's time I left to seek my revenge. I have to find H-I-J. He killed my parents."

"H-I-J's dead. He died with His Excellency. I was there. I was there at the private banquet. The assassin pumped His Excellency full of bullets, then turned the gun on H-I-J. I saw it all. So you don't have anything to worry about."

"H-I-J's not dead."

"But I just told you he is."

"You're lying. You've been lying to me ever since I set foot in this hellhole."

"I don't know what you're talking about. I've never lied to you."

"You're a goddamn communist!" I stood up and threw my tray on the floor, scattering shredded lettuce bits and minced tomatoes everywhere.

"But you don't understand, Boy Genius."

"I understand fine. You were so disgusted by His Excellency that you became a commie bastard out of sheer spite. You wanted to get back at Him, and this is the way you found to do it. I totally understand."

"Is that why you want to leave? Because I'm a communist?" he said in a wounded voice.

"I don't care about your sordid indulgences. Do whatever you'd like for the masses. I have to find H-I-J."

"His Excellency made it seem like every problem in society stemmed from communists. Anyone who disagreed with him was dismissed as a communist. Instantly, they were discredited and reviled. You know exactly what I'm talking about. You helped to expose a lot of so-called communists."

"I don't care. I don't care about class struggle or redistribution of wealth. I don't care about Fidel or the revolution. I don't care about the masses."

"You don't mean that."

"Sure I do. His Excellency may have turned against me, but it was your so-called masses, the damn proletariat, who turned their backs on me and let me become forgotten. As far as I'm concerned, they can all eat cake and die."

"They were afraid. People who were labeled communists disappeared. Then there was all that propaganda. You, of all people, should remember that."

"Look, Lucky Chang. I'm not the only one in this room who helped spread propaganda for that regime, so don't give me this I'm-more-righteous-than-thou act, okay?"

"You're right. You and I both share complicity. We both helped ruin many lives."

"Then don't talk to me like you're better than me. 'Cuz you're not."

"I'm sorry. I didn't mean anything. I promise I won't ever do that again. Just please calm down."

"I don't get it, Lucky Chang. Why is it so damn important for you to hold me here? Can't you understand that I don't want to be here? I've spent enough of my life in dark basements. It's awful."

He stepped right up to me and stared intently at me for a long moment. Then he said, "You and I are the only two true geniuses left in the world. We're kindred souls."

I began laughing. "Kindred souls," I repeated. "You and I may both have been on TV, but we're not kindred souls. We never were, and we never will be. I'm the real Boy Genius. I'm the one who deserved to stand in front of the cameras with Choco Joe. You were nobody. You were nothing. If His Excellency hadn't turned against me, you'd still be gutting fish in Cheju Island. We're not kindred souls!"

His face dropped. He turned away from me and started to clean up the mess on the floor. When he'd scooped the tacos back on the tray, he got up and said, smiling, as if nothing had happened, "Why don't I bring us more Indira? We can both use a hit. Then we'll laugh and be happy all afternoon."

"I don't need Indira. And I don't need your help anymore. I'm going now. Thanks for helping me get back on my feet. Goodbye." I began walking toward the door.

From behind me, he shouted, "Stop! Please stop!"

I paused, then turned around slowly. Lucky Chang was holding a gun aimed right at me.

"I will shoot you, Boy Genius. I don't care if you were a national treasure. I will shoot you. Just like they shot the citizens of Kwangju. Just like they shot Punk Leader Park and his wife."

His hand was shivering. I turned back around and took a step toward the door. Then another.

"Please, Boy Genius, don't make me shoot you."

I was just two feet from the door. I didn't turn around. I took another step. The gun went off behind me and a piece of shrapnel ricocheted off the wall to my left.

I reached for the door, opened it, and stepped outside. Behind me, I could hear Lucky Chang whimpering like a little boy.

CHAPTER 36
South of the Border

Dr. Namumanu appeared at her doorway wearing a bright red kimono. As always, she was holding Dr. Kyoko. Immediately, Dr. Kyoko began barking at me. Despite this warm welcome, I managed a weak smile.

"Good Spleen Man, where have you been? Everyone think you die already. Why you never call? Why you never send one postcard?"

"It's a long story. I don't really want to get into it right now. I came because I need your help, Dr. Namumanu."

She shook her head. "No can do, Good Spleen Man. Dr. Namumanu no gonna do any favors for you no more. You not a very good man. No man who is good gonna do what you do to poor wife and daughter."

"Daughter?"

"See? Good Spleen Man no even know he own child. What kind of father not know like that? Shame on you. Shame, shame, shame."

I snatched the dog from her arms.

"What you think you doing, Good Spleen Man?"

I wrapped my hands tight against Dr. Kyoko's neck. The dog began to whimper. "I will snap your dirty dog in half if you do not listen to me. So pay attention."

"You become very violent man, Good Spleen Man. Very, very violent. So much anger for no reason. Why be like that? Why not be happy? That better for your spleen."

"Shut up and listen, you quack. I'm looking for one of your old patients. He had a scar on his cheek that said H-I-J. Tell me where I can find him."

"Dr. Namumanu no can help you. All patient information strictly con-fi-den-tal. No can give information away like free lunch. That part of Hippochristmas code at Tchien Zhien Institute."

"I don't care about confidentiality or your stupid code. Tell me where I can find the man I'm looking for or say goodbye to your dirty little mutt."

"I told you already. Dr. Namumanu no can help you."

I punched the dog in the face.

"Stop!" Dr. Namumanu shouted. "Why you gotta do like that? Dr. Namumanu about to explain Dr. Namumanu no have no file here. Good Spleen Man's ex-wife Rosalyn have all file. So you barking up wrong door. Now give back precious Dr. Kyoko to Dr. Namumanu."

I handed the poodle back to her. She caressed it as if it were her own baby.

She then looked up at me and said, "Dr. Namumanu want you to know she never like you from the beginning. From very beginning Dr. Namumanu know you all wrong for Rosalyn. Why you think Dr. Namumanu spend so much time checking on her? You no think Dr. Namumanu actually like spend time with you, do you, Good Spleen Man? Rosalyn very sweet and kind. She too good for you."

I pushed Dr. Namumanu and her stupid dog into a closet and propped a chair to lock the door.

"Your spleen no good, Good Spleen Man! It sad and weak just like you!" Dr. Namumanu shouted through the door.

I hopped on one of Dr. Namumanu's dozen vintage Harleys and headed outside. Before leaving, I left a note on the fridge telling the cleaning lady to grab all the cash she could find in the house and take the day off.

The night air was cool and the roads were empty. It felt good to be outside again.

In no time, I was in front of the house Rosalyn and I had

shared. It didn't look nearly as large as it once had. Still, it'd been the first house I'd ever lived in which I could call my own. Prior to that, I'd lived in cramped concrete boxes loaned out to me on a monthly basis by clever entrepreneurs. To my surprise, the name on the mailbox read "Clarkson." I had to hand it to Rex, he'd taken no time to step in as my substitute.

No lights were on in any of the windows. I tried the front door, but it was locked. It was clear that Rex was working diligently to make sure that his new family was well-protected. I made my way to the side of the house. No windows were open on the ground floor, and the only way in was through a second-story bathroom window. As I'd done in my wild-dog days, I scaled up a drainpipe and climbed inside.

The bathroom was immaculate. Nothing was out of place, and there wasn't a single loose strand of hair on the floor. Whoever Rosalyn had hired to take care of the house was doing a fabulous job.

I slipped out to the hall and tiptoed into the room which Rosalyn had claimed as her workspace. I turned on a small desk lamp and went through her file cabinet. I looked under H, then I, then J. There was nothing.

"What are you doing?"

I turned around. A little Asian girl wearing light blue pajamas was standing in the doorway. She was holding a stuffed purple dinosaur.

I held up a forefinger to my mouth, then said, "Don't be afraid, little girl. I'm a friend of your daddy. I've come to get some papers that belong to me. So don't be afraid."

She came closer to me. "Are you very poor?"

"Why do you ask that?"

"You smell bad. Mommy says poor people can't shower or sleep well because they're bad. And Dr. Namumanu says poor people should be rounded up and sent to Puerto Rico."

"Dr. Namumanu said that?"

"Sure. She says a lot of things. She comes here all the time and plays with me. She has a dog, Dr. Kyoko, who's going to have puppies soon. Dr. Namumanu is going to give me one. Then we'll surprise daddy with her. Daddy loves dogs."

"Do you like puppies?"

"I love them. I like all animals. I'm going to be a veterinarian when I grow up."

"What's your name?"

"Clarity."

A hand suddenly yanked her back. I looked up. Rosalyn, wearing a white bathrobe, was standing behind her.

"Mommy, it's a friend of daddy's," said Clarity.

"I know, honey. Now you go on upstairs and go to bed. I'll see you in the morning. Mommy will stay here with daddy's friend."

Clarity waved to me and disappeared up the steps. Rosalyn shut her eyes for a second, then shook her head.

"Hello, Rosalyn."

"I knew it was going to be like this: you breaking into the house in the middle of the night, scaring Clarity."

"Clarity's a nice name."

"What do you want?"

"I'm looking for information on a man with a scar on his cheek that says H-I-J."

"I should have known it'd be something like that. Look under S, for scar. He came to see Dr. Namumanu back in Hiroshima. Dr. Namumanu asked him if he wanted the letters removed, but he said no. It was just a few months before you came."

I found the file. There was an address in Santa Cruz.

"Now, will that be all or do you have other houses to break into tonight?"

"Rosalyn, I'm sorry about all this. I never meant for things to turn out like this."

"Save it, Boy Genius."

"How are you and Clark doing these days?

"That's none of your business. But if you have to know, we're happy. More happy than I ever was with you."

"I'm sorry."

"Don't be. It was all for the best. I can honestly say that you were a terrible husband and I'm sure you would have been a lousy father."

"I didn't want things to be like this, but His Excellency shot me. He sent his goons to kill my parents. I'm on my way to get revenge."

"You're so pathetic. You know that none of that is true. Your parents died in a fire."

"That's not true. I thought Rex killed them, but it was H-I-J. His Excellency was behind it all along."

"His Excellency had nothing to do with it and you know it."

"You don't know what went on there, Rosalyn. You don't know what His Excellency is capable of. You can't know."

"Why? Because you're so special and I'm so ordinary?"

"No, that's not what I meant."

"Then what? Because I'm a princess and you're a working-class hero? Because your father shined shoes for a living while my dad went to work in a suit?"

"Rosalyn."

"You know, I was upset when you first walked out on me and Clarity. I wondered if it was something I did wrong. Then it hit me. All your moody silence. All your anger. I realized what they were about. It was envy."

"I've never been envious of anyone in my life."

"Sure you have. Did you ever stop to think what kind of person you would have been if your parents had been successful after they had moved here? If they had somehow managed to save a little money and buy a little house for themselves?"

"His Excellency took our money. His Excellency banished us from Korea."

"Give it a rest. Your family didn't move to the U.S. for political reasons. They were just two poor people who wanted to make some money. Had they succeeded, you wouldn't be the miserable person you are today. And you definitely wouldn't have created this fantasy world for yourself."

"I can't go back and change things. I can't go back and change history."

"You're so damn pathetic. You've completely deluded yourself into believing that you really are fighting some kind of little war. I hoped you'd change. But you haven't. You're still the angry little boy you've always been."

"You don't know anything. You don't even know that you're sleeping with a dog. You didn't know that, did you? Your husband is a dog. A mangy wild dog who used to douse old men in gasoline and light them on fire."

"Get out of here before I call the police."

I turned around, went down the stairs, and walked out the door. Rosalyn was no longer my wife, and I could not in good conscience say that I was Clarity's father. In a few years, Dr. Namumanu would give her the same operation I'd had. Then, Clarity and I would walk right past each other as complete strangers if our paths ever crossed. Perhaps it was best that way.

Before I left the driveway, I took one last look at the house. High above me, the light in Rosalyn's window went out. All was dark again.

CHAPTER 37

The Alamo

I raced up the Pacific Coast Highway on Dr. Namumanu's Harley. The road snaked through tortuous turns, but I never hit the brake once. I wanted to move as fast as I could. I wanted everything to move as fast as possible.

Rosalyn had tried her best to convince me to give up my private war, but I knew better. Those who had sided with His Excellency had to pay, and war was the only answer. War would come, and people would join the struggle by the millions by throwing their TVs out the window and murdering their landlords. To hell with Rosalyn and her precious life. What did she know about anything? She had been a sellout as a child and she was still a sellout. She would live her happy life and write me off to her therapist as a mistake which resulted from her parents' inability to express their emotions. She didn't know me. She'd never known me.

Five hours later, I was in Santa Cruz. The address led me to a large amusement park next to the beach. The large green neon sign above the entrance said, "WELCOME TO THE ALAMO."

I strolled down the boardwalk past a dozen Chinese portrait painters. I recognized some of them from the streets of Hiroshima. From the way they sketched listlessly on flimsy makeshift easels and the desperate way they sucked in smoke from their cigarettes, it was clear that they too had been exiled from their native land.

I continued on past a dozen carnival booths filled with the

usual carnie fair. An African acrobat stood on his head, balancing on top of his partner. In the adjacent stall, a Hindu fakir pierced himself with long curved daggers.

A midget, who was standing on stilts and using an orange soccer cone as a megaphone, shouted, "Come see the wonders of the ages! The freak show of all freak shows. The bearded baby and the world's largest rat. The man with three heads and the boy who talks out of his rectum. You've never seen freaks like this, my friend. Never even in your wildest dreams."

Someone dressed up as a giant rat nodded to the midget and grabbed me by the shoulders. "Read your future?" he asked.

"Excuse me," I said.

He stared long and hard at my forehead, then said, "You're going to be a father soon."

I laughed out loud. I had long ago learned that the past could be changed with very little effort, but one's future was fixed in stone.

I continued on to the end of the boardwalk. Inside a rusty cage, there was a hideous black rat the size of a St. Bernard with thick needlelike hairs jutting out of its body.

In the adjacent cage was the world's fattest woman. Next to that cage was a Chinaman with three heads and a boy with a growth on his back that looked just like Mao Tse Tung. That was followed by a cage in which a man drove a nail through his hand. I moved on to the very last cage at the far end of the boardwalk.

The cage seemed to have been forgotten. Inside, an old black man was sitting with nothing but his underwear on. His hair was gray, and his fluffy white beard stood out sharply against his dark skin. Over him was a sign that read, *"The World's Darkest White Man."*

The man behind the cage looked up at me. His eyes were covered with a greasy film, like the kind that one finds on rotting fish. Despite that film, his large, feverish eyes gazed intently into mine. In them, there was a glimmer of recognition. He lifted his bony hand and saluted me.

I knew then that the man in front of me was Choco Joe. He had aged considerably, but there was no mistaking it. It was Choco Joe, the only true friend I'd ever had.

The cage wasn't locked. I stepped inside and lifted Choco Joe in my arms. He was surprisingly heavy, as if his bones had already turned to stone. He touched my shoulder and pointed to the sea.

When we got to the water's edge, Choco Joe pointed to the ground.

"You want to lie down, Choco Joe?" I asked.

He nodded, then coughed dryly, convulsing his entire thin frame.

I set him down gently and said, "I can't believe it's really you, Choco Joe. After all these years, it's really you."

Choco Joe leaned into my ear and said, "I'm dying, Boy Genius. I don't have much time."

"What're you talking about, Choco Joe? You're as healthy as ever. And I'm here to take care of you. You're gonna live to a hundred-and-five."

He coughed some more, then said, "I turned hundred-and-six three days ago."

A stocky Mexican man walked past us carrying an icebox. "Cold soda! Cold soda!" he shouted.

Choco Joe pointed to the man. I rushed over and got him a Mr. Pibbs. He downed it in less than ten seconds, then handed me a letter written on a piece of graph paper. "I meant to give this to you sooner. I wrote it a long time ago, but I couldn't track you down, kid."

I began reading the letter.

Hello Boy Genius,

How're you enjoying your new life in the good old U.S. of A.? Have you had a chance to catch the Braves play yet? Anyway, I wanted to write to you to say I'm sorry I didn't have a chance to say good-bye to you. I wanted to see you off at the airport but . . . well . . . you know how things are here at the station. Anyway, the show's still doing well but frankly, it's not the same without you, old pal. Lucky Chang's just not that sharp and everyone here is beginning to question his credentials, though we're not supposed to say that.

By the way, they've increased my salary and I'm planning to move to a bigger house sometime at the beginning of the new year. As for the rest of the country, there was some anxiety a couple of months back, but now things are looking bright. They got rid of the curfew and we can stay out all night on the streets. Did I tell you I've met a nice Korean girl named Yunmee? She wants to marry me. Imagine that, huh? Choco Joe, the family man. It doesn't sound too bad if I have to say so myself. Take care, Boy Genius.

Your friend,

Choco Joe

P.S. I thought I could write to you without telling you this, but I must get this off my chest. You were right about me. I was a spy. But that doesn't mean you and I weren't true friends. It was simply my job to monitor events at KBS. Anyway, through my contacts I have finally learned the details of your dismissal. Those closest to His Excellency insinuated that no one was smart enough to plot an act so devious and intricate—not even the Americans—except for perhaps the smartest person in the world. H-I-J said that even if such a person wasn't the culprit, wasn't there something very strange that such a smart person couldn't foresee the unfortunate tragedy or take measures to prevent it? I'm so sorry, Boy Genius. Please forget all that's happened. Be good to your parents. There's no substitute for home and family.

"This is what happened?" I said.

"It's what happened, kid. I wish it hadn't gone down that way, but it did. But you gotta put it all behind you now. It don't make no sense to go on fighting when the war's over. Fighting only brings death and destruction. It's time to start living again."

"I can't, Choco Joe."

"You gotta. Remember what I always taught you. Two rights don't make a wrong."

"I can't."

"You can. And you gotta. Promise me, Boy Genius. Promise me you'll give up your search for H-I-J."

"I can't."

"Fighting's futile. We can't beat 'em. They're too strong. They've got allies everywhere. So promise me before I die." He squeezed my hand tightly.

"Fine, Choco Joe. Fine. I give up. I give up."

"Promise me."

"I promise, Choco Joe. I promise."

He smiled the way he'd done at KBS. All his teeth were gone and his gums were black, but his smile still managed to convey joy. Then, he collapsed on the sand.

I held up his head. "Choco Joe, are you okay?"

A tiny red dot appeared in the middle of his forehead, and a stream of dark red liquid oozed out slowly.

I turned to the boardwalk. Three men in black suits were crouched behind a wooden bench. All had rifles pointed straight at me.

I lifted Choco Joe's limp body up in my arms and ran for the sea. Bullets ricocheted at my feet and sand splashed all around me. I dove into the water and swam toward the horizon, towing Choco Joe behind me. The waves were big and strong. I flailed my arms and kicked my legs desperately. Choco Joe's body weighed me down. I had no choice but to let go of him. The second I did, he sank to the bottom like the brave soldier he'd always been. It was then that I realized just how wrong General MacArthur had been. Old soldiers *did* die; they sometimes got shot or even drowned at sea.

Without Choco Joe's dead body to drag me down and with renewed resolve, I swam like I'd never swum before. Each stroke of my arm carried me across three miles of waves. I outswam sharks and other creatures of the deep. Without a compass, I navigated by blind faith and clung desperately to Choco Joe's last words.

I would live, for I was the only one left who remembered what he and I had lived through. I was the only one who remembered Choco Joe and Aunt Six and my parents. I was the only one who knew what had happened to Rex and Lucky Chang. I owed it to myself to go on. I owed it to myself to live for the first time without the hand of governments and politics dictating my every step. I owed it to myself to live as an individual free from the tyranny of ideology. Like the explorers of old, I was headed to a New World.

I would have gone on swimming forever had I not fallen asleep. I don't know how long I slept or how far I drifted, but when I woke up, I was inside a dark room with damp walls that stank of rotting fish. Moreover, the floor was cold and wet. I reached into my pocket for a lighter and, by its light, read the message written on the wet pink wall above me: *"Long live Kwangju! Long live democracy!"*

Stacked neatly underneath this message were two piles of slick, glossy pro-American pamphlets. It was then that I realized that I was inside the very same whale that the KCIA had once used to transport a miscreant across the Korean Channel. Staring at the gently swaying walls of flesh all around me, I couldn't help but marvel at His Excellency's ingenuity. He had managed to enlist the help of even the creatures of the sea to turn the peninsula of my birth into an efficient assembly line.

Trapped inside the whale, I survived on fish and sea water, and slaked my thirst for cigarettes by smoking the pro-American pamphlets. This left a bitter taste in my mouth, but I was an addict, and there was nothing I could do.

I wondered how long I could last in the damp darkness. The only thing keeping me alive was the promise I had made to Choco Joe. After making so many promises and breaking all of them, I wanted desperately to keep this one. It was my only way to redeem myself as a man of honor.

There was a very real chance that I would never see the light of day again. A whale's belly could very well be where I'd been sentenced to live out the rest of my life. The other possibility was that I would be transported to the man whose face had mocked me for so long, the man who served as the messenger to His Excellency the Most Honorable Park, who plotted my ruin from beyond the grave. Fueled by vengeance, I fashioned a dagger out of a fishbone and sharpened it day and night against the whale's ribs until it was razor sharp. Then, I dreamt of the day when I would shove it deep into H-I-J's heart.

CHAPTER 38
Beautiful Cheju Island

The whale spat me out onto a deserted beach where a river met the sea. I trudged cautiously across the sand to the river. Then, I followed the river upstream. From my days as a genius, I knew that civilizations and people tended to settle in river valleys.

I followed the river for many hours toward its source. It was murky and the color of mud. From time to time, a Coca-Cola can drifted downstream, sending me reassurances that I would soon see people.

At dusk, I found myself staring at a tall mountain whose outline looked just like Jesus. I knew then that I was in Bonghwa, Father's ancestral village. Immediately, I kowtowed nine times to pay respect to his clan. I then set out to find the thatched hut where I'd once met Father's hunchbacked sister.

But there were no thatched huts anywhere. Also gone were the naked children running free in the streets and the large orchards carpeted with rotting apples. In their place, there was only a tall modern high-rise that looked down at the river. On the side of this edifice, there was a sign that said, *"New Village Suites."*

I straggled through the parking lot toward the entrance. A large black German sedan was parked directly in front. I couldn't help but wonder if the car had been stolen from a North American ghetto.

Inside the lobby, a young man in a black suit met me. He didn't have to say a word. I knew who had sent him, and I followed him to the elevator. As we rode up to the top floor, I felt discreetly in my pockets for the dagger I'd carved in the whale's belly.

The elevator opened into a spacious room with magnificent

views of the river. A man was seated with his back toward me. He didn't bother to turn around, but I knew who it was. My guide led me out of the elevator then disappeared just as quietly as he had appeared. I was left alone with H-I-J.

"Look out there, Boy Genius." He pointed to a cluster of buildings to his left. "This was a village of straw huts before we got here. Now, it's nearly indistinguishable from Hawaii. Do you know that this is now one of the favorite destinations for Japanese tourists? They come here by the thousands. We provide them with gambling, prostitution, and most importantly, a very favorable exchange rate." As always, his voice was devoid of emotion.

"Why'd you bring me here, you son-of-a-bitch?"

He turned around. He was a handsome old white man, but the scar on his face was still as prominent as ever. H-I-J.

He smiled slightly and said, "It's good to see you too, Boy Genius. It has been too long. I see that you too look a little different now, but I can tell you're still the same person. Fierce as ever. I trust that you were able to meet with your old friend Choco Joe. How did that go, by the way? I bet you were shocked to learn that he was a CIA operative. Or did you already know that?"

"You didn't have to go through all this trouble just to kill me."

"What makes you think I want to kill you? That's the last thing I want. It's quite the opposite. You've been chosen."

"I'll never do anything for you or His Excellency ever again."

"Don't be silly, Boy Genius. You and I both know that His Exellency is dead. If you haven't yet heard, he died like a mangy dog."

I lunged at him with my fishbone dagger, but could do no damage. Before I had taken two steps, a bullet struck me in my leg at the exact spot where His Excellency had shot me. I fell to my knees.

H-I-J pointed to the ceiling. There were armed sentries in every corner suspended by piano wire, and their guns were pointed right at me. He then shook his head and said, "Is violence the only answer you know, Boy Genius? Have you not learned anything from your many years abroad?"

"Go to hell." I threw the dagger at him. Bullets shattered it to dust before it ever reached him.

H-I-J stepped closer to me. "You are still as stubborn as ever. I see why His Excellency was so enamored of you. When I was younger I thought it strange, but as I grow older it dawns on me more and more clearly. A boy like you can be refreshing when one is surrounded by yes-men." He waved his hands at his sentries above us. "Very refreshing, indeed."

"Whatever you've planned, I'll have nothing to do with it. I'd rather die."

"But you haven't even heard what it is. How do you know how you will react? Do you know yourself so well that you know who you'll be in the future?"

"I know I'll always loathe you."

"Even if I offer you a reunion with the only two people who've ever mattered to you?"

"The only two people who've ever mattered to me were butchered by you and your men. But I will see them in the afterlife."

"An afterlife? Surely you joke. You're far too smart to entertain thoughts of such a thing. You don't really believe in a heaven and hell, do you?"

I didn't say anything. I wanted to believe in a heaven and hell, but my genius wouldn't let me. There was no evidence that our souls went anywhere after death.

"I didn't think so," said H-I-J smugly. "As for this so-called butchering, I offer you an alternative. They were not butchered. They were never butchered."

"You're a liar."

"Am I? I say to you that your parents were not killed. You have known this all along. You have even seen them." He turned to a wall and clapped his hands. A television screen that was less than an inch thick slid down from the ceiling. A film began to play. It was the same musical about Yi-Sun-Shin which I had seen many times in Lucky Chang's basement. "You have seen this film, have you not?"

"What does this film have to do with anything?"

"It has everything to do with all that's happened. This film was made in North Korea by your friend Lucky Chang. He defected to the North and made several propaganda films for them. I'm surprised you don't know this. It was all over the newspapers at the time. General Chun was furious and demanded that he be returned, while Mr. Kim's representatives calmly denied any knowledge of the defection. Lucky Chang's films weren't too bad. They were mostly what you would call melodramas. Some would dismiss them as sappy tearjerkers, but Kim apparently saw in them what lay at the heart of Korea as a nation and a people. We are a people who know what it truly means to lament and cry. For us, to truly feel sorrow is to be. Anyway, dictators really do make the worst producers. They are so very demanding. Mussolini tried to do a similar thing, you know. He commissioned Frank Capra, an American, to make a film about his life. An epic, naturally. Capra turned him down—most reluctantly, of course. Lucky Chang's films played in theaters in North Korea and at several prestigious international film festivals. Of course, he was not listed in the credits. Instead, Mr. Kim's son's name appeared as the director."

"I don't believe you. I don't believe anything you say."

"You don't have to. Here's the proof right before your eyes." He clapped his hands again, and the image on the screen froze before my eyes. "There, in the back, dressed as two deckhands. See for yourself."

Mother and Father were on the screen, scrubbing the deck of the boat.

"They were supposed to return to Seoul. Everything had been arranged. They were tired of the war you were waging. They wanted to return to be with their families and to live out their remaining days among those who remembered them. They had never wanted to leave here. It was you who wanted to go. They contacted me. They said they wanted to return home but you wouldn't let them. They sounded afraid."

"I don't believe you. I don't believe any of this."

"This isn't a matter of belief. We're talking about facts. People and events. I helped your parents make certain arrangements. I was quite fond of them, you know. They were good people, your parents."

"You didn't even know them."

He shook his head. "But I did. I knew them from the war. Surely your parents have told you about the war. They were just children when the North attacked. We were all about the same age. We played together as children."

"I don't believe you. I don't believe anything you say. There was no war. My parents never lived through any war. If they had, they would have been strong—strong enough to turn their lives around and make mincemeat of whatever came at them. But they didn't. They folded and gave up. They were weak. The war was nothing but an excuse they made up to console themselves."

H-I-J shook his head. "You're free to have your delusions, and I'm free to have mine. But the truth is the truth, independent of our disagreements. I agreed to help your parents return to Korea. In exchange, they would donate their sperm and egg. It was foolish, but we were desperate. You see, allowing you to leave was a grave mistake. It cost me my career. President Park was so sad afterwards, even though he had given me his consent. He could be such a difficult man. He blamed me for everything. I hoped to create another genius, better than Lucky Chang, to take the place of the one that had left, to take the place of you. I don't know why I did it. It wasn't as if President Park was around to tell me I did good. He was long gone by then. You see, you're not the only one haunted by him."

"I hate Him, and I hate you."

He didn't seem to hear me and continued, "Everything went according to plan. The attack. The fire. We even managed to fight off your wild dog friends. Everything was very convincing.

As for the bodies you saw hanging in your room, they were imported from Chen Zhien. You can literally buy anything there. Your parents were free to return home. You thought they were dead. They had made a clean break. But then the plane disappeared. It flew where the American fighter planes were battling the Russians. Then the Japanese and the North Koreans got involved. Your parents were let out in Pyoungyang, where the plane made an emergency landing before it took to the air again and got blown up. They appeared in two dozen magnificent films before they passed away last spring."

He handed me two plain metal urns. "I'm sorry. We didn't mean for things to turn out like this."

I clenched my teeth and climbed to my feet. On the floor, there was a puddle of my blood. I held up the urns. "Will you help me throw out their ashes?"

"Sure."

He helped me to the window overlooking the water below. He clapped his hands and the windows parted open. A gust of wind slapped me in the face. In the distance, I could make out the whale that had transported me across the ocean, heading back out to sea. I wondered who it had been assigned to ferry next.

"I liked your parents very much, Boy Genius. They were good people, honest and hard-working, never given to complaining. Quite admirable, if you stop to think about it. There are not too many like them left anymore."

I opened an urn and thrust its content out the window. The ashes floated down toward the water below.

I handed the empty urn to H-I-J. He offered me his hand in condolence. I held it tightly and jumped into the river, pulling H-I-J with me. In the second it took us to hit the water, I heard a barrage of gunfire behind me and I saw the faces of all those whom H-I-J had tortured and killed over the years including thousands of students and reporters, Choco Joe, Rex's army of wild dogs and puppies, and Mother and Father, the only two honest people the world had known since the days of Job.

Once we hit the water, I held on tightly to H-I-J and the metal urns. The urns pulled us lower and lower. H-I-J struggled to free himself, but I held on. Soon, he stopped moving. I put the urn over his head and watched him descend slowly toward the bottom. There, under the dark murky water, no army of thugs would protect H-I-J. In no time, fish would feast on his flesh and grow fat while he melted into nothingness.

CHAPTER 39
Why Did the Buddha Cross the Road?

I let the river carry me back out to sea, then swam east. Blood from my leg attracted sharks and other predators, but the stars shone on me and I didn't have to fight for my life. I attributed my good fortune to Choco Joe, whom I was sure had spoken to the partisan armies of the sea on my behalf.

Strangely, I felt no different than before I had killed H-I-J. Granted, I had placed too great an emphasis and too much hope on the single act of personal and political assassination, but I hadn't quite readied myself for such a letdown.

Once I crossed the Bering Strait, I continued east on foot, following the secret trails that had been forged by my ancestors. I retraced the footsteps of Genghis Khan's cousins down Alaska and across Canada's wintry plains. I walked and walked, moving one frozen leg in front of the other. Always, the memory of Mother and Father drove me ever forward. I had dragged them to a land that always remained foreign to them, and I was solely responsible for their demise. Mother's pained expression appeared to me everywhere. In contrast, Father surrounded me with his absence. I longed to hear his voice, the voice of a feudal serf who had never quite grasped that he no longer had to scream into the telephone to make himself heard. In its place was merely a hollow silence.

Wanting desperately to punish myself, I followed the example set by the ancient mystics of the Hermit Kingdom. Three pine needles served as my breakfast, lunch, and dinner, and I quenched my thirst by sucking the morning dew out of the air. I walked all day. At night I lay awake, searching the sky for a constellation that wasn't the visage of Mother, Father, or His

Excellency the Most Honorable President Park. Haunted by these visions and unable to sleep, I prayed to my ancestors. "Forgive me, I am that I am, for I have sinned. Against Father and Mother and the spirit of our ancestors."

But my ancestors didn't deign to help me. Just like His Excellency, they turned their backs on me and told me I was dead to them. I had become a genius without a home or a past, orphaned not only from my parents but from 200 generations of peasants who had scratched a living from the earth.

In an empty stretch of road that ran next to a railroad track, I turned to the sky and shouted, "Is the rotting flesh on my leg just a delusion, Rosalyn? Is the cold that sweeps up from the tundra just a figment of my imagination and of my sick and twisted mind? You know so little, Rosalyn. You may know things I cannot even imagine about velour and duvet comforters, but I know about wars of attrition and the power of the will. Life is more than just flesh and the physical. There are apparitions and visions, and people can be killed by more than just bullets and torture. And the most important war that has ever been fought in all the annals of history is over the territory of our minds. That you do not know. You never knew and you never understood. That's why you're in L.A. with Clarity, whose name should be Murky or Obscure or even Blind, and I am here in this freezing hell calling your name and talking to myself. You're to blame for this. You and your stupidity. No matter how many birthday parties and sweet sixteens you throw her, she'll never be the happy child you want her to be!"

Shiny automobiles fresh from Japanese plants in Mexico City raced past me, but I didn't bother trying to hitch a ride. Just as His Excellency had once held a country together through the sheer power of His will, I vowed to cross a continent with my will as my only mode of transportation.

The soles of my shoes wore thin and my eyes began to deceive me, but I kept moving forward. I would get home even if it killed me.

Suddenly, a town arose on the horizon, nestled under the tracks of the elevated 7-train. A town whose streets were filled with the laughter of children and the smells of the Third World. A town whose alleys were filled with proud children fathered by revolution and mothered by the love of women and the haughtiness of poverty.

I had been born in Seoul, but Bogota was my home. It was in Bogota that I had first tasted the engulfing flame of combat and it was in Bogota that I had first hit upon the idea of becoming a Son of the Mayflower. I celebrated and cried out in joy. I danced every dance known to man and sang the songs that had been sung by my forefathers.

I wandered my heimat seeking every chance to reminisce. But gone were the dark alleys, familiar faces, and abandoned lots. Nothing was the same. During my long absence, Bogota had been bought up by profiteers. They had repaved roads and painted over graffitti. The railroad tracks where I had howled with wild dogs were no more. Gone were the stacks of old tires and the VW Beetle on cinder blocks. And gone were the two mounds of earth where Mother and Father were buried. In their place was a trendy coffee shop and a large colorful sign for Frappuccinos.

I walked up to a payphone and dialed 9-1-1.

"Hello?" a woman said on the other end.

"I turn myself in. I'm Boy Genius Number One who used to believe that His Excellency was a god. I've returned to Bogota after many years on the road. I killed my parents and made so many people suffer. But I repent. I'm so sorry for everything. I'll run with no more wild dogs. I will cause no more trouble. I promise to be a good father and husband. I'll follow orders and do as you say."

"We don't have time for jokes, sir!" the woman shouted, then hung up.

I put the phone down and looked up. Directly in front of me was the very tenement where I had grown up. The King George

Luxury Apartments. I went inside and pressed all the buzzers on the intercom.

"Who is it?" several muffled voices blared through the intercom.

"It's me. Open the door."

The door buzzed and I pushed it open. I turned right at the lobby and pressed the button for the elevator. The lights above the elevator door lit up. It was coming down. 4, 3, 2, 1. I opened the door and got inside. It still stank of urine, just the way it had when I was a boy. And on the wall, it still said, *"Kill Mordechai."*

I got out on the sixth floor and made my way down the dark hallway. I'd been wrong about Bogota. Everything was the way it had always been. Apartment 6G. Home.

I rang the doorbell.

"Who is it?"

"It's me, Mother. I've come home at last."

The door opened and out stepped Mother with a loving smile. "Hello, Boy Genius. You look so tired. Come on in. You should get some rest. It's been a long strange journey, hasn't it?"

"It has, Mother. And I've missed you so much."

"Your father's in the bathroom. He's going to be so happy to see you."

I stepped inside and sat down in Mother's kitchen. Mother rushed to the stove to heat up some food. I hadn't tasted her cooking in many years, and my mouth watered in eager anticipation.

Father stepped out of the bathroom in his underwear and shouted, "Is that you, Boy Genius?"

"Yes, Father, it's me. I've come home at last."

I hugged Mother and Father and breathed in their scent, the smell of soybean paste and the brown earth of Bonghwa. I had come home. I had come home at last.

"You were wrong, Rosalyn. I didn't imagine the whole thing. They killed my parents. But I got 'em back and I got 'em back good. I killed H-I-J, and if His Excellency were alive, I would have killed Him too. My parents loved me despite my genius. You never loved me like they did. You never loved me at all."

CHAPTER 40
Throne of Gold

"Walk to the light at the end of the tunnel, soldier!" a voice shouted.

I did as the voice commanded. I knew now how important it was to follow orders.

Waiting for me at the end of the light was not General MacArthur, but my father, the Prince of Bonghwa and a genius in his own right. He had grown a long silver beard that came to a point near his belly since the last time I saw him. It suited him well.

He greeted me with open arms. "You're home at last, my son. We've been waiting for you for a long time now. Come. Join your mother at my side for you have entered my heavenly kingdom. Here, you shall not want for anything and you shall not suffer from any pain, not even from your memories. You are finally home."

Mother appeared next to him. She hadn't aged at all.

"Mother!" I ran to her.

She hugged me tightly and buried her face in my chest. "My son. My precious, precious son. You're home at last."

"Mother!"

She bent down before me and started to wash my feet with her tears. "You've come home at last. We're so sorry for trying to run away. We shouldn't have done it. We should have stayed put next to you. We're so sorry."

"Stop it!" Father shouted. "Don't tell the boy we're sorry. This is the kingdom of heaven where there is no sorrow and regret. If anything, son, we're sorry you couldn't join us earlier. All your worries are in the past. Forget them and enjoy the now. Live and rejoice for you are in the Garden of Eden before the fall of man and the temptation of Satan."

Above us, three golden angels blew on shofars and Father's ancient voice echoed through the clouds. "Behold, here is my son, whom I love. The Prince of Peace, the King of Gooks, the King of Kings."

I smiled. I was weary and weak, but I was finally home. Then, for the first time since becoming a genius, I wept, and my tears joined those of my aunts who had cried for my mother at an airport on the other side of the world when His Excellency was still alive and I was just a boy.

OTHER SELECTIONS IN THE **AKASHIC URBAN SURREAL** SERIES:

***Manhattan Loverboy* by Arthur Nersesian**
(author of *The Fuck-Up*)
"Nersesian's newest novel is paranoid fantasy
and fantastic comedy in the service of social
realism, using the methods of L. Frank Baum's
Wizard of Oz or Kafka's *The Trial* to update
the picaresque urban chronicles of Augie
March, with a far darker edge . . ."
—*Downtown Magazine*

> 203 pages, paperback; $13.95
> ISBN: 1-888451-09-2

***Fast Eddie, King of the Bees*
by Robert Arellano**
"A lively and imaginative 21st-century parody
of the Victorian novel of the foundling in
search of his true parents, complete with
comically elaborate twists and turns of plot,
broad social satire, and a rich cast of
characters. *Fast Eddie*'s a lot of fun."
—Robert Coover

> 235 pages, paperback; $14.95
> ISBN: 1-888451-22-X

YONGSOO PARK is a filmmaker and playwright who was born in the mountain village of Bonghwa, South Korea. A Van Lier fellow at the Asian American Writers' Workshop and a graduate of Swarthmore College, he wrote and directed the independent feature film *Free Country*. He and his wife live in Harlem, New York.